BODYGUARD'S BITE

HOWLER BROTHERS BOOK 2

SILVIA VIOLET

1

STORM

I was standing at the bar, drinking a club soda and speculating with Charlene, the bartender on duty, about the lack of crowd that night. I'd considered going home since things were so slow and two of my brothers were there to keep an eye on things. They didn't really need me—not that they let me do all that much anyway. They were as protective of me as they would be of a pup. Just because I was a submissive didn't mean I couldn't take care of myself, settle disputes, or run this club as well as any of them. But try telling that to an older alpha brother. Yeah. That never worked.

Charlene said something else, but I didn't hear her because a dark-haired, bearded man who pushed all my buttons walked in from the side entrance. He must have a VIP pass if he didn't enter from the front, but I knew most of the VIPs, and I'd never seen this wolf shifter before. There was no way in hell I would've forgotten him.

He was fucking gorgeous, and the way he carried himself —confident without looking arrogant, comfortable like he felt good in his own skin—had me salivating. His smell was earthy and comforting and crazy strong for me to detect it from across the room. He was exactly what I'd been looking for: a man who made me want to kneel, who might be willing to work me over the way I wanted without being afraid my brothers would come after him.

If he was as strong as he looked, he had no reason to fear them. He wasn't as tall as King and Bryce, who were both several inches over six feet, but his shoulders were broad, his chest wide, and his arms... I shivered as I studied them. There was no question he could hold me down easily. His hair was dark and buzzed short. I'd need to be closer to tell if his eyes were dark too. Maybe I should go find out.

It had been far too long since I'd been with a man and even longer since I'd seen someone who called to me like he did. When you have overprotective brothers, finding a Dom to play with can be a challenge, and when your family owns the best kink club in town, it's even worse. The last few times I'd tried to arrange a scene for myself, I'd been cock-blocked by King, the oldest and most high-handed of my brothers.

I needed to act fast before they realized what I was up to. I'd have to convince this gorgeous man to leave with me. If I tried to get us a private room here, King would be alerted. He'd start grilling the guy, and most likely, intimidated or not, the hot-as-hell stranger would decide a fun night of cropping my ass wasn't worth the trouble. Thankfully, having so many brothers had taught me one good thing —how to speak up when I wanted something. I might be a sub, but I knew what I liked, and I wasn't afraid to ask for it.

I sat my drink down on the bar and got Charlene's attention. "Hopefully, I'm about to get out of here. Do not tell my brothers." She looked like she was about to protest. "I'll text them, but I seriously need to get laid, and they'll fuck it up."

She grinned. "Deal, but what do I tell King if he asks where you are?"

"Tell him you talked to me, but after that you don't know where I went because you had to get something from the back."

She stared at me for a moment. "But I don't... Oh." She surveyed the bar. "Hmm. I do think we're running low on oranges and limes. I'd better go in the back and restock."

"You should. I'd hate for you to have to serve someone a margarita with no lime slice."

"Exactly. Now go get your man. Are you after the guy that just came in? The one you were staring at?"

"Maaaybe."

She snorted. "You should be. He's fucking hot."

I growled, my wolf coming to the surface.

Charlene held up her hands. "Whoa. I'm not planning on poaching or anything—unless you find out he's straight. Then you can send him my way."

I forced myself to smile as I tried to figure out why I'd reacted so strongly to this man before I'd even spoken to him. I couldn't be sure he was into men or a Dom or that I'd even like him.

Mine, my wolf said, and fuck. I wanted him to be. "Sorry. Just feeling a little possessive tonight."

Charlene rolled her eyes. "Go get laid. You're right. You need it."

Without another word, I slid from my barstool and turned to find the man I was determined to have. He'd been admiring the men and women on the dance floor, probably contemplating whether to join them, but as I approached him, he turned toward me and held my gaze.

"Let's go somewhere quieter," I shouted when I was close enough that he might possibly hear me over the music.

I led him down a hallway, praying none of my brothers were in the security booth watching the cameras. I kept going until I reached an emergency exit at the end of the hall. If we stood just to the side of the door, we'd be out of sight of any of the cameras.

The man raised his brows. "What are we doing here?"

"Talking. For now."

He looked slightly perplexed.

"What were you hoping I'd suggest? Fucking in the alley?"

His mouth opened and closed, and he shook his head. "No, I…"

"I want something more interesting than that, and I'm assuming you do too, or you wouldn't be here."

"I'm here to look around, get a feel for the place."

I knew I would have remembered him if he'd been here before "This is your first time here?"

"Yes."

"Then how… Never mind." It didn't matter how he'd gotten a VIP pass. All that mattered was whether he wanted what I did. I really hoped so because just his scent had me so hard I thought my cock might split my pants. "I have an idea."

He smiled. "What is it?"

"We go to a hotel, you spank my ass until I'm begging you to stop, and then you hold me down and make me take your cock as hard as you can give it to me. I don't need anything elaborate. Just good, rough sex with you in charge."

He blinked at me and licked his lips. "I… um…"

"Oh shit. Are you a Dom? I assumed because of the way you carried yourself and how you were watching me, and…" I knew better than to make judgements like that. People often assumed I was a Dom because I was one of the Howler brothers.

"No, you were right. Or, well... I like to be in charge. I don't have much experience beyond being a natural control freak, enjoying telling my partners what to do in bed, and the occasional spanking. All of this"—he gestured toward the scenes we could see being acted out through the entrance to the public playroom—"is new to me."

"But you must have a VIP pass, unless... You didn't sneak in did you?" I shouldn't have found the idea that he was here illicitly hot, but I did. The longer I went without a good spanking and a hot fuck, the more rebellious I got.

"No. I borrowed a pass from a friend who thought I would like it here. Like I said, I really planned to just observe."

The passes weren't transferable, so technically he was breaking the rules, but I didn't give a fuck. "I suppose I've derailed your plans."

He smiled, and I wanted to get on my knees right there.

"I don't mind, as long as you weren't expecting someone more experienced."

"No!" Shit. I said that way too loudly. "I'm looking for someone who would enjoy exactly what I suggested. If we were to do something more... advanced, then... Well, I take safety seriously, but right now I just... I need to get out of here, and you intrigue me."

"Do I?" He gave me that smile again, and I swear it was almost as good as him touching my cock.

Did I sound too desperate? I really did need to get fucked and spanked and maybe a hell of a lot more. I usually took things more slowly with someone I didn't know, but I'd told him what I wanted, and no way in hell was I backing down.

I laid my hands on his shoulders, enjoying the warmth I

could feel through his t-shirt. Then I leaned in close so my mouth was right by his ear. "You smell incredible, and I want you."

After tugging on his earlobe with my teeth, I leaned back and met his gaze. His eyes were unreadable as he studied me. Had I gone too far? Had I freaked him out?

"You're certainly surprising."

"Surprising in a good way?"

"A very good way." His voice was low and rough, and there was heat in his eyes. Could he possibly want me as much as I did him?

"Let's get out of here. We can get a hotel, and—"

"Wouldn't it be easier to get a room here?" he asked.

It would, but then my brothers would likely figure out I was with someone new, since I'd have to get the key. "It would be, but all the good rooms are occupied." That was a blatant lie. It had been slow all night, and chances were most of the VIP rooms were available. But I wasn't taking any chances. I was going to have this man, and no one was going to stop me.

"And you know this how?"

"Oh… um… I actually work here, but my shift is over now."

"I see." He looked like he wasn't buying my story, but thankfully, he didn't ask more questions. And I hadn't lied about working there; I'd just omitted that my family owned the place.

The man let his gaze trail over my body, then he tilted his head as if considering my offer. "Since neither of us would be satisfied with a quick fuck right here, I suppose you're right. We need to go somewhere private."

I think I stared at him for several seconds with my mouth hanging open, because I couldn't get past the image in my mind of him turning me around, pressing my hands to the wall, ordering me to stay still and taking me right there. I wouldn't even mind the risk if it wasn't for the fact that one of my brothers could discover us. If I'd been anywhere else, I might have begged for a quick fuck there as a prelude. I wasn't normally into semi-public quickies, but apparently, I was up for just about anything with this man.

"Right. Let's go." Could I sound any more eager?

The man smiled at me and held out a hand. "I'm Jax."

When I accepted his offered hand, heat raced through me. His grip was firm, and I wanted his large hands all over me.

"Hi, Jax. I'm…" I froze. If I gave him my name, he might realize who I was. Our family was well-known in shifter circles, especially among wolves. I didn't want him to know he was about to wreck the ass of Storm Howler, club owner, billionaire, and younger brother to the man who basically ran the wolf shifters and could fuck up anyone who got in his way. "I appreciate you telling me your name, but for tonight, I need to remain anonymous."

He gave me a slow once-over. "Are you in the witness protection program or something?"

I grinned. "No, just protective of my identity."

"You could've just given me a false name."

"I didn't want to do that."

"Thank you. I appreciate your honesty." That was the moment I realized I might want a hell of a lot more than a rough fuck and a reddened ass from this man. I didn't just want him. I *liked* him.

Mine, my wolf said again. I closed my eyes and took a shuddery breath, needing to get my animal side under control. My wolf loved pain and pleasure as much as I did, but he'd never been this possessive before. What was going on?

When I opened my eyes, Jax was staring at me. His eyes

had shifted to wolfish yellow, and I would've sworn I could feel his wolf right at the surface. He growled. "I think we should get out of here now."

I agreed, but I was pressed against the wall, fighting the urge to tilt my head to the side and bare my neck for him. I wanted the scrape of his teeth and the weight of him against me. But not here. He turned to head back down the hall, but I grabbed his hand. "Not that way. I... um... I'm actually skipping out a little early, and I don't want my boss to see me." King liked to think he was the boss of me, so in a sense, that was true.

Jax glanced toward the emergency exit. "We can't go out this way either. What do you suggest?"

"Promise you'll wait right here? I'll only be a minute."

"I'm not going anywhere."

Great. Now my cock was harder than ever, which made it difficult to hurry like I wanted to. I had no doubt I looked ridiculous scurrying off toward the supply room with a raging hard-on, but it was worth it. I found the magnet we'd used to keep one of the emergency exits from alarming when it malfunctioned a few months ago. Thank fuck it was still there. Then I grabbed a bottle of lube and some lotion that was perfect for soothing a reddened ass. Finally, I retrieved my bag from where I'd stashed it in my office and hurried back to Jax.

I opened my palm to show him the magnet. "I can use this to keep the door from alarming. I just—"

He held up a hand. "I've used that trick several times."

"Oh, okay." I wondered why he'd need to slip through an emergency exit, but I didn't ask. He waited patiently for me to disengage the mechanism. Once we'd slipped out, I let the door close carefully, pulling the magnet out with me at the last second. I breathed a sigh of relief when the door latched and no alarm sounded.

"Where's your car?" I asked Jax.

He gestured to the right. "It's the black SUV at the end of the row."

As we walked quickly toward his vehicle, he glanced over at me. "I would suggest we go back to my place instead of a hotel, but I'm staying with a friend. I'm only in town for a few days."

"Oh, that's no problem, and we can't go to my place. I have… roommates." I lived at the family estate with all of my brothers. No way in hell were we going there. "Also like I said, I take safety seriously, so I don't go home with strangers. I'll pay for the hotel, since it was my idea."

"That's not a problem. We can split the cost."

"No. It's my treat."

He opened the passenger door of his SUV for me, and I climbed in. I didn't usually accept rides with strangers either, but I wasn't about to call one of my family's drivers to pick us up. All my instincts said that this man was safe.

He's perfect, my wolf assured me.

He was, and I wanted to tell him my name. I wanted to hear him use it as he fucked me. Did I dare take that risk? "So you're not from here?"

"No, this is my first time in town. I got out of the army a few months ago, and I've been at odds figuring out what I'm going to do next. My friend let me know about a job opportunity out here. He insisted I come check it out, so here I am."

Former military. That explained the buzzed hair and the way he carried himself like he could do anything. "What did you do in the army?"

"I was special forces. I spent the last few years leading one of the two shifter units."

Fuck, he just got hotter every second. And now I understood why he knew how to disarm a door. "Where were you stationed?"

"All over, but most recently in the desert. It was... I'm glad to be stateside again."

"I bet." I didn't even want to think about the harrowing things he'd likely seen and done. "Since you've never been here, I guess you don't know much about the shifter community."

"No. I've mostly been out of the country for the last few years, so I don't even know much about the shifter community back home."

Surely it would be safe to tell him my name then.

He frowned. "What's wrong?"

I was usually better at masking my feelings, but he had me all stirred up. "Nothing. I just... since you're not from here, I was thinking... My name is Storm."

He cranked the engine as he turned to look at me. "That suits you."

"It does?"

"Yes. I'm guessing tonight isn't the first time you've shown up out of nowhere and derailed anything in your path."

Heat filled my face. "I can't say you're wrong."

"And these curls are..." He reached out and touched my hair, which often looked like a storm had passed through it. I leaned into his touch and sighed. He pulled away far too quickly. "Tell me where we're going."

If I were with someone who knew me, I would go to the best hotel in town, but since it was five hundred a night for their smallest room, I chose a still nice, but less prestigious, option. A few minutes later, Jax pulled up in front of the hotel. He intended to drop me off and go park, but I shook my head. "Let the valet get it. It'll go on the bill."

"I really can't let you—"

"I've had a good year at work. Let's treat ourselves." All my years were good, but he didn't need to know that.

He narrowed his eyes and studied me in a way that made me shiver. "You're awfully bossy for someone who claims to want to be controlled."

"Maybe you can take care of that once we're upstairs."

He grabbed my wrist, gripping me firmly enough that I'd have to struggle to get free. "There's no question I can handle you. I may not be experienced with all the toys and equipment they use at Tooth and Claw, but I assure you, I know how to make a person do what I say."

My mouth opened and closed, but no words came out.

"Get out of the car and go check us in while I park."

"Yes, sir," I replied in a deliberately breathless voice.

"Don't get sassy with me. I'll make you regret it."

Dear God, the way Jax could go from gentle and accommodating to controlling was going to be the death of me. A really fucking good death.

I slid from the car and waved off the valet who was headed our way. Forcing myself not to look back, I entered the hotel, but before I approached the registration desk, I pulled out my phone and sent a quick message to our family chat, letting my brothers know I'd left the club for the evening and would not be home tonight. I assured them I was perfectly safe and told them that if they bothered me, I would find a way to make them pay. I would catch hell for this tomorrow, but I already knew Jax would be worth whatever imperious lecture King forced me to sit through.

JAX WAS WAITING BY THE ELEVATORS WHEN I STEPPED AWAY

from reception with our room card. As I walked his way, he pressed the call button, and the elevator door slid open.

"Which floor?" he asked as we stepped inside.

"Eighth."

He tapped the right button, and the door slid closed, trapping us together. It wasn't a long ride, but he watched me the whole time like he was ready to devour me. By the time the elevator dinged to let us know we'd reached our floor, my cock ached, and I was gripping the railing so hard my knuckles were white.

Jax grinned when my wobbly legs made me fall against him. "This is going to be a very fun evening."

"Um… yeah. It… it is." I was already wishing he wasn't just in town temporarily.

He took the envelope that held our key, laid a hand against my lower back, and steered me in the right direction. "I love how easy it is to render you speechless, especially considering you were quite talkative back at the club."

I was practically floating as we walked to the room. The last few times I'd been with a man had been enjoyable, but I had felt somewhat distant from the proceedings.

The Doms I played with knew what they wanted, and so did I. We satisfied each other's needs, but they never could have made me fall apart with only a heated glance. The sexual tension between me and Jax was stronger than anything I'd felt in a long time.

I'd been more carefree in my late teens and early twenties, but after my father died and King took over the family empire, we made a lot of enemies. My brothers were right to be concerned about me. There were people out to hurt my family, and many of them thought my brother Shadow and I were easy targets because we weren't alphas or Doms.

Shadow didn't go out much. He'd been through hell as a

teenager before we adopted him. He was still recovering, but I was no fucking target. Still, a willingness to stand up for myself didn't equal the physical strength my other brothers possessed. Jax wasn't a threat though. I knew that, and my wolf did too, so I was going to let myself go. I deserved to revel in pleasure at least for one night.

2

JAX

I slid the key card into the door, waited for the green light, and then motioned for Storm to enter ahead of me. My gaze fell to his round ass, shown off so well in tight gray dress pants. I was going to enjoy stripping him, working him over, reducing him to cries and moans, too far gone to respond with sassy comments. I could give him the roughness he craved, and maybe, if the job interview I had in the morning worked out, I could see him again and try out some new things with him. I was already certain that one night wasn't going to be enough to quench my thirst for him.

I closed the door behind me, intending to make my usual check of the room's possible exits before telling Storm exactly what I expected of him tonight, but this wasn't a simple hotel room. It was a large suite with a separate living room and bedroom and a bath nearly as large as my bedroom back in Boston. From the soft carpet that began a few feet past the door to the upholstered sofa by the picture window that looked out onto the city, everything screamed luxury. The room looked like one where I'd rescue a diplomat or a wealthy asset, not one I'd stay in myself.

"Do you like the room?" Storm asked, sounding concerned.

"It's very nice, just not the kind of place I'd usually stay. All we really need tonight is a bed, though the floor would do, or a wall would make a decent substitute."

Storm sucked in his breath, and my dick appreciated the sound. "The bed would be more comfortable, but I'm up for any or all of those options."

I studied him until color rose in his cheeks. "You asked for me to take charge, so I'll decide where I'm going to have you and how."

Storm ran his teeth over his lower lip. "I did ask that, didn't I?"

I prowled toward him, holding his gaze. "You did."

His hazel eyes widened, and his lips parted with a soft moan. I loved how expressive he was. He made no attempt to hide his desire.

"I like being told what to do, but I don't surrender easily. My… job has forced me to learn to be more aggressive than I might be naturally."

It was more than his job. I was sure of that. Something about his life circumstances had caused him to learn to be assertive when he needed to be—not that it was a bad thing. I wanted to know more about Storm, though I knew I should respect his desire for privacy. He obviously had money and privilege. Should I recognize him? Was he someone famous? He'd said he worked at the club, but something had seemed off about that. He'd certainly known his way around. When he'd left me by the emergency door, I'd watched him closely enough to see that he'd gone into the supply room and then an office. Maybe he was friends with the owner, King Howler. He was the man I'd be interviewing with the next day. From what my friend had told me, King was very wealthy and quite powerful. I'd done a cursory search to learn more about him, but he might as well have been a ghost for all the concrete information I could find. If I was offered the job, I had a hacker friend who could help me find out more, but I didn't want to bother him if the situation didn't feel right.

"I can push past your resistance if that's what you want. In fact, I'd enjoy it."

"I'd enjoy it too."

"Good. What's your safeword?"

"I'm really boring. I use 'red' to stop and 'yellow' to slow down."

I trailed my fingers down his arm. "There's nothing boring about you."

He licked his lips. "Thank you."

I slid my fingers into his hair, loving that his loose curls were as soft as they looked. Then I let my hands slide free and trailed my fingers over his cheek and down his neck, relishing the warmth of his tanned skin. I'd spent most of the weeks since I'd left the army holed up at home. I felt directionless and out of step with everything. Then I'd seen Storm and felt a connection that pulled me to him. It was like I was waking up for the first time in weeks. "Strip for me."

Storm's eyes widened.

"Don't make me wait."

He sank his teeth into his lower lip. The way he went from self-assured one moment to uncertain the next only made me want him more. I couldn't wait to find out how responsive he'd be when I got my hands on him—or better yet, my cock inside him. My wolf growled, urging me to pick up the pace. If I let him have his way, he'd rip Storm's clothes off and shove him down on the bed. But I'd promised Storm more than just a hookup, and I always delivered on my promises.

I enjoyed power games, and I wanted to push this beautiful man until he let go and quit trying to control how I controlled him. I could force him to obey. I could break him if I wanted to, but I didn't. I wanted to make him feel, to make him need. I wanted to work him over until he collapsed in an exhausted, fucked-out heap.

Most of my recent encounters with men had been about the release of tension or the need to work off an adrenaline rush. In the army, there hadn't often been time to indulge in games.

Storm obeyed my command and peeled off his dress shirt, revealing tanned skin and a smattering of hair across his chest. He paused, looking up at me through his absurdly long lashes as he reached for the fastenings of his pants, and I had to slide my hand past my own waistband and rearrange myself as my cock grew fully hard.

"Keep going."

He held my gaze for a few heartbeats before he popped the button and slid the zipper down very slowly. He knew how to tease. Was he pushing me intentionally, hoping I'd get rough with him, shove his pants down and push him to his knees? "How rough do you want me to be? I don't want to go too far. I've been trained to be aggressive, to push until I get what I want, but I don't want to go too far with you."

"Shifter special forces, huh? That's so hot. I guess you could like, kill me eighteen different ways with a toothpick."

I couldn't help but laugh. "Maybe not eighteen, but certainly a few. It's easier to just use my hands though."

Storm grinned. "I'm not afraid to use my safeword. I'll stop you if you go too far."

"Good. I expect you to. I don't want you to be afraid of

the fact that I know exactly how and where to touch you to control you."

Storm smiled. "I'm not afraid. Don't treat me like I'm fragile. I get that from my family and anyone they approve of me being with." He froze suddenly, and I guessed he'd revealed more than he meant to.

"You don't have to tell me anymore. You're an adult. You asked me for what you wanted, and I'm going to give it to you and trust that you'll stop me if you need to."

"Thank you for trusting me."

I was more determined than ever to give Storm what he craved. "Before we start, tell me what else you like."

"I like pain, so you can spank me hard. I like to be humiliated a little, like being called a slut or told I'm just there to be used, and sometimes I like to pretend I'm being forced."

It was as if he'd read my mind and found all my favorite jerk-off fantasies—ones I'd wanted to act on but never had. Pain. Humiliation. Force. All turned me on and made me come hard and fast.

"But what I like most is being told what to do and expected to obey. I want to be able to get out of my head and let my responsibilities go."

I'd guessed that. Storm was a pleaser who was in desperate need of having his own needs met, even if those needs involved him obeying. What mattered was that this was about his fantasy. It was what he'd asked for. "I can give you that."

"Then do it."

I gripped his chin, forcing his head up and making him look at me. "I give the orders, and you obey them."

He groaned, and I slid my hand down to pinch his nipple, loving the startled sound he made. "More of that, please, sir."

Storm was baiting me with his sass, so I ignored it,

knowing I could punish him for it later. "I want you naked. Now."

He pushed his pants over his hips, revealing silky black briefs that clung to him, leaving nothing to the imagination. I flexed my hands, fighting not to grow claws. My wolf wanted to shred that tiny garment so it fell right off him. I told the beast to be patient. This wasn't a fucking race, even if it had been a while for us.

Want. Take. Claim.

No. That was... Claiming was for mates. This was just sex. It wasn't... And yet, Storm seemed like he'd been made for me. And his scent. I'd never smelled anything more intriguing. Could he be my... No way. I was just imagining things because I was way too fucking horny. Storm was gorgeous, and he challenged me just the way I loved. That was it. There was no deeper reason for my reaction to him.

He toed off his shoes and then pulled off his socks and pants, leaving him wearing nothing but those absurdly alluring briefs, which probably cost more than everything I was wearing. He held my gaze as he reached for them, hooking his fingers in the waistband.

"Stop," I commanded. He obeyed instantly, which sent a thrill through me. This was going to be such a good night. "I'll take those off you myself."

"When are you going to undress?" he asked, letting his eyes roam up and down my body. "I want to see you."

And because he did, I was going to make him wait. "You will. But not yet."

"But I—"

"Who's in charge here?"

"You are."

"That's right. And I want you to stand there with your hands clasped behind your back and your eyes closed."

"I…"

"Storm."

"Yes?"

I stared at him, knowing that was all it would take.

"I'm sorry. I'll… I told you I'm not good at—"

I tweaked his nipple hard enough to make him hiss. "Fuck."

Enjoying his reaction, I flicked my thumb over his other nipple, letting him sense the threat. "Are you going to be good?"

"Yes, please. Yes… Do you want me to call you 'Sir'?"

"What does it mean to you to call me that?"

Storm chewed his lip for a moment before answering. "It means I'm surrendering to you and you're taking control, but you're also taking care of me."

"Then yes, I want to be 'Sir' to you."

"Yes, Sir." This time, there was no mockery in his breathless tone.

I sank to my knees, and Storm gasped. I waited for him to protest again. When he remained silent for several seconds, I took hold of his briefs and tugged them down just enough to expose the tip of his cock. My wolf was so insistent that I take Storm now that I barely managed to keep my hands fully human.

Storm's underwear was as soft and silky as it had looked. It had to feel wonderful sliding over his cock. There was a damp spot on the front from his precum. I leaned forward and ran my tongue over it. Damn. Even through the fabric, he tasted good.

"J-jax?"

I glanced up. Storm's eyes were dark, his pupils blown, and we hadn't even really started. He gave himself over to pleasure so easily. He was like a gift, one I wanted to be worthy of. I took a slow, deliberate breath, drawing in his rich scent of cinnamon and warmth, spice and comfort. The pleasure was so intense it made me dizzy.

Take, my wolf insisted. I would take everything Storm offered. I couldn't resist. He'd had me under his spell from the moment he'd met my gaze across the club. I pulled his briefs down farther, exposing his shaft.

"Please," he whispered.

I nipped at his hips, and he whined sharply. "Be patient."

I pushed his briefs all the way off, and he stepped out of them. When I turned my attention back to his cock, the tip was damp, and he was hard and straining toward me, like he was begging to be touched. I circled my fingers around the base and then licked the precum that was about to drip from the slit. "Mmm, you taste so fucking good."

He whimpered, and the sound seemed to vibrate through me. I'd hardly touched him, and he was already making me feel more than I had in months, waking me up, making me feel alive again, needed again. I wanted him to feel like that too, so I took his cock deep into my mouth, dragging a groan from him.

He tensed, and I was sure he wanted, needed to move. I sucked him harder, teasing his underside with my tongue. His hands came to my head, but I took hold of his wrists and pushed his arms back behind him. He whined and fought my grip. "Need to touch you. Need—"

I pulled off his cock and growled. "Keep your hands behind you, or I will stop right now. Do you want to come tonight?"

His eyes were huge. "I... yes... please."

"Then do as I say, and if you're good, then I'll let you. But don't you dare come until I tell you to."

"I—"

I slapped his thigh with my free hand. The cry he made was more like a howl from his wolf, and mine reacted, growling and pushing to be freed. I longed to release my wolf. How good would it feel to be wild, uncontrolled in a way I hadn't been in years? It was too dangerous though. I'd been trained to be ruthless. My wolf had become a weapon, and I was afraid of what might happen if I gave him more freedom. If he took complete control…

Need. Take.

Storm's knees buckled when I took his cock all the way down my throat. I gripped his hips, steadying him. I'd only meant to tease him. I thought a small taste of him would be enough for now, but he was too delicious. I couldn't stop. He trembled as I worked him. I knew he was fighting the urge to move, to grip my head again and hold me in place while he came down my throat, but he stayed still, offering himself to me, letting me take what I wanted. I was determined to draw this night out as long as I could because I didn't know when I would experience anything as pure and bright as Storm's need again.

Keep him, my wolf demanded, but I pushed that crazy thought aside. Even if I moved here, I didn't belong in this beautiful man's world. This was a one-night deal.

I slid a hand between Storm's legs, and he automatically widened them for me. I teased his balls, testing the heft of them, feeling how high and tight they were. He was close. I wanted to bring him right to the edge. I wanted him to have to fight to hold himself back. He needed that struggle.

I reached farther back and skimmed my fingers over his hole, making him cry out.

"Please. I'm going to come. I can't —"

I pulled off, leaving him shaking and gasping. He stumbled, catching himself on my shoulders. I gripped his waist, holding him up. "I've got you."

"I know."

His words seemed to reach inside me and squeeze my heart. He trusted me when he had no reason to other than instinct. I wanted more than anything to take care of him, to give him what he needed

Protect. Mine, my wolf insisted, but Storm was only mine for the night.

"Position yourself on the bed, ass in the air, head against the mattress."

"Um... I..."

He was still leaning on me for support, and I guessed he was questioning whether he could walk to the bed. "I thought you were strong enough to take whatever I gave you."

He glared at me. "I am."

"Then walk to the bed, and do as you were told."

He pushed off my shoulders and glared at me again, then he turned and obeyed. He didn't even sway as he moved. I loved how damn determined he was.

3

STORM

I forced myself to stand up straight and walk toward the bed, even though my vision was fuzzy around the edges and my cock ached like Jax had been tormenting me for hours, not minutes. Jax wasn't babying me. He believed I was strong, and I wasn't going to disappoint him. I knew my brothers didn't really think I was helpless, but my father had, and I barely remembered my mother. No one had ever had the kind of confidence in me that Jax had. It was like he knew exactly what I needed.

The room seemed much bigger than it had earlier. I had to focus on putting one foot in front of the other until I reached the bed. I leaned against the edge of the mattress for a few seconds before I trusted my shaky legs to hold me as I yanked the comforter off. I didn't want to have to explain to the hotel staff why it needed to be replaced. When I'd exposed the silky sheets, I climbed up, barely managing to do so without toppling over like an idiot.

I worked to slow my breathing as I positioned myself near the end of the bed, arching my back and sticking my ass up. I wanted Jax to be tempted. I wanted him to consider driving right into me in one rough push, because he was right—I could take anything. I turned my head to the side and pressed my cheek against the cool sheets. Then I reached back, gripped my ass cheeks, and pulled them apart, exposing myself for him. I was rewarded with a sharp intake of his breath.

"I like how eager you are to have your hole stuffed, but it's going to be a while, so unless you want your hands slapped, you need to put them up by your head. In fact, you probably want to get a pillow and wrap them around it. You'll need something to muffle your screams."

Holy fuck, that might be the hottest thing anyone had ever said to me. I had to bite my lip to stop myself from telling Jax all the ways I wanted him to make me scream. I wanted to surrender, but it was so hard to let go. Despite being held back from some of the more dangerous aspects of my family's businesses, I was used to spending my day managing people, sorting out issues between employees, smoothing ruffled feathers of club patrons, and checking in on our other businesses. Making sure everything ran smoothly was my job, but not tonight. Tonight that was Jax's responsibility, and it was my responsibility to obey. I grabbed a pillow, stuffed it under my head, and let myself sink into the mattress as I exhaled.

"That's right. Relax and enjoy." Jax stepped up behind me and squeezed my ass, pulling it apart the way I had. "I'm going to give you exactly what you asked for." My mind spun, cycling back through our conversation at the club.

I'd asked him to spank me so hard I had to beg him to stop. I had a moment to wonder if I'd made a mistake before his hand cracked down on my ass.

He didn't give me time to process the blistering sting before he spanked me again. He was not holding back. He'd taken me at my word that I wasn't fragile, and I fucking loved it. I arched my back more deeply, asking for more. And he gave it.

His hand came down again and again, every single blow harsh and punishing. He didn't tease me. He didn't wait for me to catch my breath. He just sent hot, stinging pain across my ass until it was burning so badly each smack became a momentary relief from the flames shooting across my skin.

I squirmed and whimpered, squeezing the pillow as my wolf growled inside. He wanted to fight, and I wasn't sure how long I could hold him back. Claws shot from my fingers, and I dug them into the pillow. Shit. This wasn't good. I had to control myself better.

"Am I making you lose control?" I was relieved that Jax's voice was teasing, not angry. "Aren't you strong enough to hold your wolf inside?"

"Fuck you," I snarled.

He smacked me even harder, and I cried out, my wolf still fighting to take over. He wanted to shove Jax off me and take what I wanted from him, force him to bury his cock in me. My own cock was so hard I wondered if I could come just from the blows against my ass. I didn't want Jax to stop, and I was afraid he would if I couldn't find better control, so I used all the concentration I could muster to make my wolf back off. My hands became human again, and I was no longer biting into the pillow with fangs.

"That's good. I'm proud of your restraint."

Jax was proud of me. He believed in me, and that made me want him even more. My cock was leaking so much precum there had to be a damp circle under me on the sheets. I glanced over my shoulder and caught his gaze. "I can take anything. Do your worst."

He snarled, and I felt the prick of his claws against my

flaming hot skin. I was sure I bore the imprint of his hands on my ass, but he didn't hold back. He raked his claws over me. I didn't think he'd actually broken the skin, but my ass was so sore already it felt like he was ripping me apart. I squeezed my eyes shut, trying to hold back tears, but I couldn't stop my whimpers.

Jax laid a hand at the base of my spine. His touch was warm and gentle, and it soothed me despite what he'd just done.

"More?" His voice was as gentle as his touch. I wanted to reassure him I was truly okay, that he was doing everything exactly right. No one had ever made me feel like this before, pain and pleasure perfectly spiraling together, taking me out of myself, but I didn't know how to say all of that, so I just said, "Yes, please."

"Such a good boy." He slid his hand slowly down my spine. I arched up, seeking his touch, but he pulled away and spanked me again.

"Fuck, that hurts!" I cried.

"It's meant to, but you can take it."

I could. I could do whatever he wanted me to. He kept the blows coming, and I reached a point where I couldn't hold back my tears anymore. I let them flow down my cheeks as he brought his hand down more slowly now with long pauses between each strike. It was hard to relax as I waited for the explosion of pain. The sound of his hand smacking my flesh echoed in the room. "Please."

"Please, what?"

"I don't know. It's so good. Too good. Too much."

"Five more."

I could do that. "Yes."

"Count them," he commanded.

That I wasn't sure about. My brain was foggy from both

the pain and pleasure. I felt far away and also right in the moment, as if nothing existed but his hand and my sore ass. He smacked me again. I opened my mouth, but nothing came out

"Storm?"

"O–one."

Another blow came down right on top of the last one, making me sob. It hurt so bad. I needed relief. I needed to come.

Jax pinched my ass, and I cried out. "Count for me. You can do this."

"Two."

He slapped my other cheek twice, one smack right after the other.

"Three. Four."

"That's good, Storm. I'm so proud of you."

I held my breath, knowing there was one more. Jax dug his hand into my sore cheek, pulling at the flesh. "Please," I begged. "I can't."

"You can," he insisted before giving me the final blow.

"F-five."

I'd done it. I'd taken it all. Was he going to fuck me now? I knew he wouldn't be gentle. He wasn't going to treat me like I might break, which meant it would hurt like hell. My ass was on fire, but that only made it better. I wanted it to hurt when he filled me up. I needed him to own me, inside and out. I needed his knot, his cum. "Need you."

"I know you do, baby. You need me right here." He teased the edge of my hole, making me suck in my breath. "You don't even care how much it's going to hurt. You're such a slut for me."

"Yes! I'm your slut, and I'll do anything for you."

"You'll take my cock all the way inside without any prep?"

I groaned. "Yes, please. I'd love that."

"You're so fucking eager, so needy."

"For you."

He brushed my sweaty hair off my forehead, leaned over me, and skimmed his lips along my hairline. "You're so gorgeous like this, surrendering to me, taking a harsh spanking. Do you remember your safeword?"

"Red. That's it, I mean. I'm not saying it. I–I want what you said. Your cock. No prep."

He smiled down at me. "I know you do, and you've done so well. You deserve it."

"I can be so good for you." As I said the words, I realized I didn't just mean that I could hold myself still and take the harshest spanking I'd ever had. I didn't mean that I could let him fuck me as hard as he wanted to. Those things were true, but I meant so much more. I could be good for him, and he could be good for me. It was like we were made for each other, almost like we were… *mates.* When my wolf said the word, a shiver ran through me.

But it couldn't be. I wasn't going to trust myself—not even the instincts of my wolf—when I was floating so high in subspace. Jax seemed perfect in that moment, and that's why my mind was trying to convince me we were fated for each other. I couldn't let myself hope that was true.

"Are you comfortable in this position?" Jax asked.

"I can stay in any position you want me in."

He pressed his lips along the outer edge of my ear. "I believe you, but that's not what I asked. I want you to be comfortable enough to enjoy what comes next."

How could he be so tender and so harsh at the same time?

"Yes. I want to stay like this, ass in the air, hot and aching. I want you to take me, to own me."

He growled, and I rose up on one elbow so I could turn and see him better. His eyes had shifted to lupine, and I could feel the animal inside him. I wasn't scared though. I liked knowing he was close to losing control.

Our lips were close, just inches apart. I didn't usually kiss the men I played with at Tooth and Claw. It felt too intimate, which seemed strange considering what else I was letting them do to me, but kissing was different. The pain, the bondage, the rough fucking was all about needs, but there was something so personal about the touch of lips. I wanted that closeness with Jax.

I looked into his eyes again and brushed my thumb over his lips. "Please."

He kissed me then. I wasn't sure if he'd understood what I was pleading for or if he simply needed it too. He was careful at first, almost tentative. It was so unlike the way he touched me before. Then something seemed to break open, and he was kissing me savagely, teeth raking over my lips, tongue thrusting into my mouth. His beard abraded me, and I cupped his cheek, wanting to feel it against my hand. I felt consumed by him in a way wholly different from how I'd felt as he'd spanked me.

When he finally pulled back, we were both desperate for air. We watched each other, and I felt a cautiousness between us that had not been there before. Was he feeling the need for more the way I was?

Mine, my wolf insisted. I wanted that to be true, but was there even a point to me trying to have a relationship, considering who I was, who my brothers were?

Before I had a chance to worry more about that, Jax brushed the backs of his fingers over my cheek and said, "I'm going to fuck you now, hard and rough like you asked. You're not weak or fragile, and I know you can take it. I know you want to be stuffed full of my cock. You want to writhe and beg. You want to hurt."

My mouth was devoid of moisture, and my pulse pounded in my ears. "I… I can. I do. I… Yes."

His eyes stayed wolfish as he rose off me, standing once again. The bed put me at the perfect height for him to drive into me. He gripped my sore ass cheeks, and I whimpered. "Your skin is so hot it's almost burning me. It must hurt like hell."

"It does. It's glorious."

He gave a low chuckle and began to strip. I watched over my shoulder, transfixed as he lifted his shirt over his head, revealing his broad, hairy chest and his beautifully defined abs. He must have had a serious workout routine in the army, and it showed. He unfastened his jeans and pushed them down, and I gasped. He wasn't wearing anything underneath them, and his cock sprang free. It was huge, long and thick, and I stared at it hungrily.

He wrapped his hand around it. "Is this what you want?"

"Goddess, yes."

He grinned as he kicked off his shoes and stepped out of his pants. "Don't move. I need to get the lube. It's in your bag right?

"Yes." Had he seen me put it in there? Or had I told him and just didn't remember? Why did I care? He was back in a second. As I heard the wet sound of him slicking his cock, I imagined how it was going to feel stretching me, making me burn both inside and out until I forgot everything but pain and pleasure. I wanted to be taken, to be used, to be trusted to be strong enough. His cock was right there, the tip pressing against my hole. I held myself rigid as I waited. Then Jax slapped my ass, making me yelp as pain burst across my skin. He didn't pull back, he left his hand pressed against my tender flesh. That seemed to make the blow reverberate through me. "If you tense up like that, it's going to hurt more. Breathe and open for me."

"I don't know if—"

Another blow on my other cheek. "Fuck."

"I don't want to hear you say 'can't' about anything. Now breathe."

I inhaled deeply, feeling my body expand with the air. I couldn't disobey him when he spoke with that tone, which held demand, concern, and pride. I let the air out, and when I was about halfway through my exhale, Jax thrust into me, forcing the last of my air out in a whoosh.

I struggled to breathe again. He was stretching me so wide. Dear God, he was fucking huge. How could I take all of him? It wasn't like he was giving me a choice though. He wasn't rough, but he kept pushing in, making my ass burn deep inside. I was too full. It was too much. I tried to pull away, but he held my hips so tightly I could barely move. When he bottomed out and his hips pressed against my sore ass, I bit my lip to hold in a sob.

"Let it out," Jax ordered. "It's okay to cry. It's okay to whine. It's even okay to beg as long as you take what I want to give you."

"I will," I gasped.

He kissed the back of my neck. "I know you will, baby."

He began to pull out slowly, and the feel of his cock dragging over that sweet spot inside me made me whimper and push back against him, wanting more. It hurt like hell, but I needed it. "Use me. Please. As hard as you need to."

"I will, baby. I'm going to give you everything you asked for."

SILVIA VIOLET

He drove back into me, and I cried out, my body jerking from the shock of being filled so fast.

"Oh fuck. I don't know if I can do this." I was sure he was going to split me in two.

"Yes, you do. You know what you're capable of." He didn't go slow this time. He thrust into me over and over with harsh, deep strokes, using his grip on my hips to tilt them at just the right angle to press against my prostate. I writhed and squirmed, working my hips and trying to push back against him.

"Need you. Need more. Please!"

"That's right. You need me to fuck you, to own you."

"Yes! I can take it. I really can."

He growled. "Damn right you can. Open that eager little ass and let me give it all to you. I'm going to give you my knot and fill you with my seed."

Oh Goddess, how big was his knot going to be? My ass felt stretched to the limit. I was already at the point where I wasn't sure I knew the difference between pain and pleasure. It was all just sensation, but how much more could I handle?

4

JAX

Storm's eager words and his desperation were driving me insane. My wolf snarled. He wanted out, so badly it felt like he was clawing at my insides. I fought it, but his words were so seductive. *Bite. Claim.* He insisted it would feel so much better if I just let him free. If I made Storm mine.

I couldn't do that. We couldn't be mates. That was crazy, but even if we were, I would never claim him without his consent.

My wolf was starved for contact. That was all. Wolf shifters needed touch, whether sexual or for comfort, and I had isolated myself for far too long. Storm was the most amazing man I had ever fucked, and I was desperate to touch, to feel. That's why my wolf thought I needed more. And who wouldn't want to be such an incredible man's mate?

Storm's ass had to hurt like hell, but he kept begging for more. I would give that to him, but I couldn't let my wolf out. He was too dangerous. If I lost control, he might damage Storm. Unbidden, memories flashed in my mind of some of the horrible things my wolf had been ordered to do during my last tour of duty. I froze as I tried to push away the images in my mind.

"Jax? Are you okay? Do you need something?" Storm was looking at me over his shoulder. His voice and a deep breath of his intoxicating scent made the memories dissipate. "I need you to turn over. I want to watch your face as you come, but your ass is going to rub against the bed, and as silky as these sheets are, it's still going to hurt."

He was already moving. "Like I said before, I like pain."

"Then lie on your back so I can give you what you need."

He held my gaze as he lay back and opened his legs. "You know you can use a safeword too. Just because you're the Dom doesn't mean you might not need to stop."

I'd never been with anyone who was so concerned for my comfort. "How are you so perfect?"

"I'm not. I just want this to be as incredible for you as it is for me."

"Trust me. It's probably better."

"Then fuck me. Please."

I pulled his legs over my shoulders and sank back inside him. He gasped as he worked his hips, trying to take me deeper.

"You like that, baby? The sheet scraping over your tender ass?"

"Fuck, yes."

I began thrusting into him again, my rhythm fast and harsh. He took it all, clinging to my arms, watching me with awe on his face. I drove into him so hard I pushed his body toward the headboard. He cried out, but he didn't stop begging for more with his body and his words. "More. Harder. Need to come. Please let me come."

"Not yet, baby."

I kept going until we were both dripping with sweat.

Precum pooled on Storm's belly, and I knew he couldn't hold back much longer. "Can you come hands-free for me?"

He narrowed his eyes. "I told you. I can do anything."

"Then show me." My knot began to expand, stretching him. He squirmed and writhed, and I kept thrusting into him as much as my knot would allow. He gripped my arms and arched his back as he cried out, finally letting go. His cock shot so hard, cum hit his chin.

The ecstasy on his face was the hottest thing I'd ever seen. *Take him. Mark him*, my wolf urged. Seconds later, I pumped out my release inside him. As my orgasm rocked me, I struggled to keep my eyes open. I wanted to watch Storm as he came down from the high of release. Sweat glistened on his beautiful body as he flopped back against the bed, cum-covered and exhausted.

When I was able to speak again, I laid a hand on his chest. "Are you okay?"

His eyes fluttered open, and he grinned. "I'm so much more than okay."

I rolled us to our sides, and he settled his leg over my hip and snuggled into me. "Comfortable?"

"Mmmhmm."

I kissed his damp curls. "You are as strong and capable as you said you were."

Storm sighed and nuzzled my neck as I wrapped my arms tightly around him. I wanted to hold him against me forever. He was caring and understanding and so fucking sexy. Dear Goddess, the way he begged. I wanted to tell him this had been so much more to me than just a chance to get off, but I wasn't sure if he wanted to hear that.

When my knot deflated, I let my cock slip from his body and gently pulled away. He'd been at least half-asleep, and he made an adorable discontented snuffle. "Where are you going?"

"To the shower. We're both a mess, so if you want to go first—"

"I don't mind mess. I kind of like it. Feeling your cum slide down my legs is so delightfully filthy."

I groaned. He was going to kill me if he kept talking like that. I leaned down and ran my tongue over one of his nipples, capturing some of the cum that had landed there. "I can handle messy, but I assumed you'd want me to get out of here."

"You don't want to spend the night?" I was surprised to see how disappointed he looked.

"That's an option?"

"I thought it was a given. We have the room until noon tomorrow. We should make the most of it."

The longer I stayed, the harder it was going to be to leave him, but no way could I turn him down, especially not when he was staring at me like a sad pup. "We could always shower together."

"No more sweaty, sticky cuddles?"

I frowned. "While I appreciate the sexiness of having you covered in cum. I had enough sweaty, unclean nights while I was in the army."

He laughed. "Then let's shower, but… I don't think I can stand to have the water too hot."

"Oh fuck. Your ass."

"Yeah. I brought some lotion we keep at the club that's really soothing. You can put some on me after we get cleaned up."

"I'd love to do that as long as you accept that touching you is going to make me want you again."

He grinned. "I'm counting on it. I assumed the point of the shower was to get clean so we could get dirty again."

"Damn, you're insatiable, aren't you?"

He slid from the bed and pulled me up with him. "I told you I was a good little slut."

We both laughed as we walked to the shower, and I realized I'd never joked around with a sex partner like that. It felt really damn good.

Despite Storm's enthusiasm, it was clear he was still a bit unsteady and really sore after our shower, so I had him lie down on the bed while I got the lotion from his bag. He was so beautiful stretched out on his stomach, the long line of his back, the taper of his waist, the bright red marks on his ass.

I squeezed out some lotion and rubbed it between my hands to warm it up so it wouldn't be too much of a shock to his warm skin. I worked it into his ass cheeks as carefully as I could. I expected him to flinch, but he arched up into my touch. "You like this?"

"Mmmm. So much."

"Doesn't that hurt?"

"It does, but it also feels incredible. I don't know if I can explain why, but you gave me something I needed, and now you're taking care of me. That's like the best thing ever. Maybe that's…"

He turned his face into the pillow like he needed to hide from me. It was the first time he'd seemed embarrassed all night.

"Storm, I love that you enjoy the aftercare too, and of course, I'm going to take care of you. I would never do this to someone and then walk away." I pressed a kiss at the base of his spine.

He let out a soft sigh and looked at me again. "I can't decide if I want to go to sleep or beg you to fuck me again."

"You could sleep for a little while and then I could wake you and see if you want more. Or we can lie here and you can tell me more of the things you like."

Storm pushed up to his elbows and looked over his shoulder. "I want to tell you everything."

Was he just talking about his favorite kinks, or did he mean more than that? Because I felt like I could tell him everything too, even things I hadn't talked about with anyone.

We held each other's gaze for a few seconds. Tension rose, and Storm licked his lips. "Um… I…"

"Yes?"

He looked away and sat up. "You know what would be fun?"

"What?" I was certain that wasn't what he'd been going to say, but I let it go. I was going back home. Chances of me getting and accepting a job offer were slim, so it was better for both of us if we kept this from getting too intense.

"Ordering room service and eating it naked on the balcony."

I smiled despite the heavy thoughts I'd been having. "That sounds fantastic."

Storm reached for the phone. "I'll call."

I grabbed the receiver from his hand. "No. I'm in charge."

Storm laid a hand on his chest and pretended to swoon. "Do you have any idea how fucking hot you are getting all dominant about ordering food?"

Did he know how fucking hot he was just existing? "I aim to please."

"You do a fine fucking job of it. You're a natural at controlling me."

"Thank you." I wanted to take charge and place the order, but I realized I didn't know what he liked. I'd forgotten we didn't know much about each other, because somehow in the short time since I'd seen him across the club, I'd started to feel like I knew him completely.

Mine, my wolf insisted again.

I pushed the thought aside. "Are there any foods you can't or won't eat?"

"I basically like everything. I'm as much of a slut for food as I am for sex. But something fried and completely unhealthy sounds really good right now."

I picked up the phone, pressed the button for room service, and held Storm's gaze as I placed an order for cheese fries, burgers, and two slices of chocolate cake.

Storm had a huge smile on his face when I hung up the phone. "You really do know how to treat a boy."

"I know how to treat myself and thought you'd be happy to go along with it."

Storm smirked at me. "Like I said. You're a natural Dom."

I stepped back in the bathroom, having remembered that this was a nice enough place to provide fluffy, terrycloth robes for guests. I grabbed one and pulled it on as I stepped back into the room.

Storm scowled at me. "I thought we were going to be naked."

"Somebody has to answer the door when room service comes."

"And you think you need clothes for that?"

I raised my brows and glared at him, but he just grinned. "Maybe your ass isn't red enough after all."

His eyes widened, but he didn't truly look daunted. I was pretty sure he'd let me spank him some more, but I wanted him to be able to walk the next day. "Take the comforter and go sit on the balcony. I'll be out there when the food comes."

"But I —"

"Are you contradicting me?"

He groaned. "Goddess, you're so fucking sexy."

Knowing I'd pleased him warmed me all over. I watched him through the sliding glass door. He stretched out on his side on the small loveseat and let the comforter fall to the floor, obviously unashamed to be out there naked. Most likely no one could see him anyway, but most people would still feel the need to cover up. Storm was a man who knew what he wanted, and he wasn't ashamed of it. That was more rare than it should be.

My wolf urged me to go to him, kiss him, taste him, take him again, but my human side was content to watch and wonder how I'd gotten lucky enough to have even one night with so perfect a man.

5

STORM

After the food arrived, Jax joined me on the balcony. I'd only been apart from him for a few moments, but despite the gorgeous view of the city from up here and my wolf's glee at being out in the night air, I'd gotten anxious for Jax to join me. Just those few minutes had been long enough for me to miss his touch.

I grabbed a fry off the tray before he'd even put it down on the small table.

He laughed. "You are hungry, aren't you?"

"I didn't eat much dinner, and you seriously wore me out."

He chuckled. "I'm not going to apologize for that."

"I wouldn't want you to. Thank you again for listening to me."

He brushed my hair off my forehead. When I met his gaze, the intensity in his eyes sent a shiver through me. "Everyone deserves to be listened to."

He cared how I felt, and he was the hottest fuck I'd ever had, better than the most well-trained Dom I'd been with. But he was leaving.

Unless he got a job offer and chose to stay…

No, I shouldn't get my hopes up.

"I don't want you to think my life is terrible or anything. It's just that when everyone around you is overprotective, it's hard to get what you want. But with you…"

We stared at each other for a moment, electric tension crackling between us. I held my breath, not sure what was happening. I refused to listen to the impossible things my wolf was saying inside me.

Then Jax grabbed a fry and held it up to my mouth. I took it from him and nipped at his finger.

His eyes widened in surprise. "Are you asking for another spanking?"

I shrugged. "Maybe."

"I'm not sure your ass can take that. You might want to think before you say too much."

Sitting up to eat hurt like hell, but the pain was a delicious reminder of what Jax had done to me. "For now, we should probably eat, but that doesn't mean the thought of being spanked by you again isn't hot as fuck."

Jax grabbed a fry for himself. "Mmm. Those are good." He ate a few more before adding, "You need to stop tempting me because I would love to feel the heat of your reddened ass under my hand again. To hear you cry and beg. Before tonight, I thought spanking was something I enjoyed but didn't need to do often. Now, I think it's my favorite thing in the world."

Jax spanking me was now my favorite thing too. "I wish you were here for longer. There are so many more things I'd like to do with you. Who knows, maybe you'd even like one of those better than spanking."

"I could end up getting a job here and…"

"You'd want to see me again if you did?" Fuck. Did I sound too desperate?

"I would. Very much."

My heart raced. Dear Goddess, let him get this job. "I'll give you my number, and if you are going to move here, let me know, and we can see what happens."

We exchanged contacts, then took turns feeding each other as we enjoyed the rest of our perfect night.

"STORM! STORM! LET ME IN, OR I'M GOING TO BREAK THIS door down."

I blinked and rubbed my eyes. Where was I? And what the fuck was going on? Was that Bryce? I tried to call out, but my voice was too scratchy. I cleared my throat and tried again. "I'm coming. Calm down."

I rubbed my eyes again and looked around. I was in a hotel room. Oh shit. Jax. Was he still here? His side of the bed was empty. I was about to check the bathroom when I realized a former special forces soldier would've already been at the door, trying to figure out what was going on.

I was trying to find some pants when I saw a note on top of my bag.

Storm,

You're sleeping soundly and I don't want to wake you. I had a great night. I'll let you know if I take the job.

Jax

I gave a silent squeal of delight before folding the note and shoving it into my bag. The last thing I needed was for Bryce to see it.

When I pulled the door open, Bryce glared at me. "You didn't check the peephole."

What the fuck was wrong with him? "I recognized your voice and your smell. Why would I need to?"

"You should always check."

I rolled my eyes. "I'm not a pup. For Goddess's sake, you're only two years older than me." I gestured for him to come in, not wanting to have a shouting match while he stood in the hall. I wasn't even sure what time it was. Not too early, based on how bright my room was, but still, none of the other hotel patrons needed to hear us arguing.

"Are you all right?" Bryce asked.

"Yes. Can't you see that?"

He glanced toward the bathroom. "Are you alone?"

"I am now."

I looked around again and saw my pants peeking out from the edge of the comforter, which I'd kicked off the bed in the night. Jax's body had been all the warmth I'd needed. I grabbed them and yanked them on. It wasn't like being naked in front of my brother was a big deal, but he was dressed, and clothes would help me feel more authoritative yelling at him for whatever absurd excuse had him chasing me down instead of calling like a normal person.

"Why haven't you been answering your phone?"

Shit. Maybe I wouldn't be yelling at him after all. I'd turned my phone off the night before, and now it was... "What time is it?"

"Ten. King's about to lose his fucking mind. I better text him."

"Ten? Wow. I never sleep that late. I turned my phone off so you wouldn't bother me last night."

Bryce growled. "Never do that again."

"If you didn't always try to cock block me by calling and texting nonstop when I go out with anyone, I wouldn't have done it last night."

He scowled. "Just because I don't want anyone taking advantage of my little brother—"

"It's not taking advantage when I ask for it."

Bryce sighed. "I know. It's just our instinct to protect you."

"Yes, you do it because you care, but it's exhausting." I pulled my phone from my bag and turned it on. I had fifty-six messages and twenty-three missed calls, all from one or another of my brothers. "I sent a family message last night. I told you I was fine."

"If you look at the time stamps, you'll see we let you be until it was time for you to show up for work. You were supposed to be there for the interview we were doing this morning. The one for the new bodyguard, remember?"

I looked down at my phone and saw that he was right. The first text had come at seven-thirty. Of course they were worried about me. I was never late for anything. "I'm sorry I scared you. I… I had a long night. When the man I was with left this morning, he didn't know he should wake me, and obviously I didn't set my alarm, since I never turned my phone on."

"I take it this was a *good* long night?" Bryce said.

"Really good."

"He was good to you?"

I hated that I couldn't keep myself from smiling like a lovesick idiot. "He was the best because he listened to what I wanted, and he only hurt me the way I like."

Bryce growled.

"Calm down. You know I'm a submissive. Our family runs a fucking kink club."

Bryce blew out a long breath. "I know. It's just… It's you."

"Can't you be happy for me?"

47

He laid a hand on my shoulder and smiled. "I am happy for you, and you look really good. You must have needed this."

"I did."

"So are you seeing him again? I expect an introduction next time."

"If I introduced you, that would mean the end of things since you, King, and Garrett would scare him off."

Bryce huffed.

"It doesn't matter though. He was only in town temporarily."

"Aww. That's too bad."

I decided not to explain that there was a chance he'd be moving here. I didn't want to get my hopes up, and my brothers didn't need to know all my business.

Bryce's phone buzzed, and he frowned at it.

"It's King, isn't it?"

"Yes. He said I better drag your ass home so we can sit you down and make sure this never happens again."

"Of course he did. I'm not sorry I wanted a night on my own. I deserved that. I'm a fucking grown-up. A grown-up who helps run multiple lucrative businesses, but I get why you were scared this morning. I would never have done that on purpose."

Bryce pulled me into a tight hug, and I drew in his comforting scent. "I know. I'm just glad you're all right, but King and Garrett probably aren't going to accept your explanation that easily, and Shadow was terrified. He was pacing around the house growling and barking. He clearly wanted to go with me to search for you, but he refused to change into human form."

I felt the worst about scaring Shadow. All my brothers loved me and would do anything for me—except give me the

48

freedom I desired. But Shadow was still working to overcome his past, and stress like this wouldn't help. "Does he know I'm all right? Is he with King?"

"He's with Garrett, and I texted them too."

"So now everyone is going to drop what they're doing and have a yell-at-Storm session?"

Bryce grinned. "Pretty much. Yeah."

"And none of you have more pressing business than this?"

"Do you honestly think King's going to be able to concentrate on anything until he manages this?"

"No. Just let me finish getting dressed and grab my stuff, and we'll get this over with."

"I'll try to sneak you upstairs so you can shower and change. It would be best if we didn't have this conversation with you smelling like your lover from last night."

I thought about the things Jax and I had done in the middle of the night. When I took a deep breath, I smelled our mingled sweat and cum. I was so not going home like this. "Damn. I wish I had a change of clothes here."

"I can run and get you something while you shower," Bryce offered.

"You'd do that?"

"Of course. There are a couple of shops just down the street. I'm sure I can find something for you." He looked me up and down. "What size are you?"

I told him and tossed him the room key.

"Get cleaned up, and I'll be back soon."

For once, I didn't mind him ordering me around. "Thanks, Bryce."

"I've always been the easy one to convince. The rest of your morning will suck, so this is the least I can do."

Even as little kids, Bryce had been the most easygoing of

us, and he was happy to do even the smallest thing to thwart King.

He was right. This morning was going to suck. I was not looking forward to dealing with the rest of my brothers. If they were just being overprotective assholes as usual, I'd tell them off, but this time, I'd actually been irresponsible. I'd worked so hard to prove that I could make my own choices, that I didn't need anyone looking after me, and now I'd fucked up and scared them all. At least I could have a few blissful moments of peace under the warm shower spray before I had to face the music.

WHEN BRYCE AND I ARRIVED BACK AT THE HOWLER FAMILY estate, the rest of my brothers were already gathered. The only one of my siblings who was missing was my sister, Lacey. She'd found her mate a few years ago—a tiger shifter to King's horror—and moved away with him.

King exploded at me the second we entered the living room. "What the hell were you thinking?"

"That I deserved a chance to go out with someone you hadn't vetted."

King pointed to the couch where Shadow was curled up in wolf form. Bryce and I sat down, and I stroked my younger brother's soft fur. He laid his head in my lap as King paced in front of us. "When were you going to bother to turn back up? You do have a job and responsibilities."

I blew out a long breath and raked my hand through my hair. I needed to be mature and apologize for scaring them, but King's attitude made me want to defend myself and tell him none of this would've happened if he treated me like an adult.

My wolf snarled, wanting to be free, and I could feel King's wolf spoiling for a fight as well. His eyes had shifted, and he'd squeezed his hands into fists, likely to keep them in human form. As invigorating as it might be in the moment, I would never beat King in a physical fight, and we'd both wind up sore and tired and just as angry as when we'd started.

So I had to stay calm. It always fell to me to be the voice of reason, even when I was the one who fucked up.

"I'm sorry for scaring all of you this morning. I turned my phone off last night when I left the club, and I should've turned it back on before I fell asleep. That's on me. It's not something I've done before, and I don't plan to make that mistake again. Can we move on now? I'd like to hear about the interview and get started on the rest of my work for the day."

"Nice try," Garrett said. "You're not getting out of this that easily, but we have a compromise to propose."

My brothers' idea of a compromise usually meant me agreeing to whatever they said. "A compromise on what?"

"You having the freedom to run off and fuck whoever you please," King said.

I growled. "Why should you have more freedom to do that than I do?"

"Because I…" Even my obnoxious, arrogant, I'm-in-charge-of-everything older brother didn't have the nerve to try to justify that. "I don't want you to get hurt."

"I know how to take care of myself. I don't play with people who haven't already proven they're trustworthy." As soon as I said those words, I regretted it, because while that had been true in the past, I'd trusted my instincts with Jax. They'd been right, of course, but I hadn't known anything about him when I'd left the club with him.

King ran a hand through his hair. "I know."

"What about last night?" Garrett said. "How did you know the man you left with was trustworthy? Was he someone we know?"

Damn him for being so perceptive. "I don't have to confine myself to only going out with men you know."

"You didn't answer the question." Garrett pointed out. "How did you know he's trustworthy?"

"I took a fucking risk for once. My wolf liked him, and nothing about him set off even a hint of wariness. Can we just get back to this compromise?"

King snarled. "I still don't like this."

Shadow lunged toward him, growling, and I tried to hold him back, stroking his sides.

King actually looked contrite. "I'm sorry, Shadow. You've already told me I'm being an ass."

"You are, you know?" I said. "I was in the wrong this morning, but you have to trust that I'm not as fragile as you think I am." Why couldn't they trust me like Jax had?

Garrett petted Shadow as he caught my gaze. "It's not easy when we have so many enemies."

King stepped forward and took my hands in his. "I know how capable you are, how strong you are. Without your ability to manage things, I could never have accomplished all I have since our father died. I value you, and I love you, so I don't want to see you hurt."

He was sincere. I could feel it and see it in his eyes.

I almost told him everything was fine and he could keep on being his arrogant, overprotective self, but the way he treated me really wasn't okay. "You know I love you too, no matter how frustrated I am with you, or with any of you." I glanced around. Shadow nuzzled me. Garrett nodded. He wasn't one for emotional displays, but I knew he loved me as much as the rest of my brothers.

Bryce laid a hand on my back. "I don't know what we'd do without you."

"Thank you all, but I still haven't heard about this compromise."

King let my hands go and glanced at Garrett, who gave him a pointed look. "You can go out with whoever you want without us interrogating you if you take one of our guards with you."

I bristled. "None of you take a guard with you."

"Shadow is with a guard or one of us anytime he leaves the house," King pointed out.

"That's different."

"It is, and it isn't," Garrett said. "You're more vulnerable than us, Storm. It's simply true, and the other shifter families know it. They also know how much we love you, so by striking at you, they would devastate us."

I exhaled. He was right, but I didn't have to like it. Was I willing to make this bargain? It wasn't what I wanted—the same freedom as my alpha brothers—but it was better than what I had now, and far more reasonable than I expected from King. The guards wouldn't interfere in what I was doing, and I could take a few more risks, knowing they were there watching out for me.

"Fine. I accept the compromise."

Bryce smiled. "This worked out better than I expected."

Neither Garrett nor King looked pleased with the situation. But they'd offered it, so now they were stuck with it. One thing I did know about my brothers: they would never go back on their word.

"I would prefer one of the newer guards though. It would be too awkward to have a hookup while one of the men who've been with us since I was a kid was potentially listening in."

King shuddered. "They are not going to listen, but I've already planned to assign you the guard we hired this morning. It would've been nice if you'd been here to meet him and give your opinion, but we all liked him. He has a military background, and he answered all our questions in a straight-forward manner, never trying to pretend he was anything he wasn't."

"He was the perfect candidate," Garrett agreed.

Shadow whined and rubbed himself against me.

"I asked Shadow to come to the interview since you weren't here," Garrett explained.

"And?" I looked at my younger brother.

Shadow raised his snout, telling me he agreed with their assessment.

When King mentioned a military background, all I'd been able to think of was Jax. If only he were the one who'd be following me around. My phone had buzzed several times while I'd talked to my brothers, but I wasn't ready to check it yet. I wanted there to be a message from Jax so badly that I was afraid to look.

"When does he start?"

"Tomorrow," Bryce said. "We explained that we needed someone right away. He said he could work the rest of the week, but then he'd need to have a few days to gather his things and move."

"So I can meet with him in the morning?"

"That's right. And if you were to need anyone tonight—" King's growl cut Bryce off.

"Tonight we will all be having dinner together," my oldest brother declared.

I wanted to protest just on principle, but I made the mature choice. "I'll be here for our weekly dinner. I don't have any plans tonight."

"Damn right you don't," King said. He may have given a little, but he was still King. Would he ever stop treating me like a kid? "Now if we're done with all this nonsense, there's work to do."

"Shall I accompany you to the club?" I asked. King glared at me for a moment. "Or would you rather lock me in my room here so you'll be sure you know where I am?"

Garrett studied me. "That's not a bad thought."

I scowled at him. "That was a joke."

"Let's go," King snarled, and I followed him out the door.

6

JAX

As I got ready to start my first day at my new job, all I could think about was seeing Storm again. After my interview had gone surprisingly well, Mr. Howler had offered me the job on the spot.

I'd gone into the interview unsure about working as a bodyguard for the Howlers because what I had learned about them made them seem cold and ruthless, but I'd seen a group of brothers who cared about each other and wanted to make things better for the shifters in their city. They were exactly the sort of people I wanted to work for. Being around them made me miss my old unit even more than I had been already. I had no family to speak of, and I wondered if I truly felt a part of something again.

I wasn't sure personal security was where I wanted to be, but I didn't have to do this forever. Working for the Howlers would give me the focus I'd been needing, and a chance to continue what I'd started with Storm. I'd told myself I'd dig up anything I could find on the family, but when they'd made the offer, I couldn't turn down the chance to see him again. I knew better than to make life decisions based on one night together—one amazing, eye-opening night—but I'd thought of him almost constantly since I'd left him the day before. As soon as I'd left the Howler estate, I'd texted him to let him know I'd not only taken the job but would be staying in town for the rest of the week because my new employer wanted me to start immediately. We'd agreed to meet for dinner once I was done with work for the day.

I'd come close to missing out on the opportunity altogether. I hadn't remembered to set my alarm until I'd been drifting off to sleep sometime in the early hours of the morning after round three—or was it four?—with Storm. He was so damn insatiable, but I'd finally exhausted him. He hadn't even stirred when my alarm had gone off. I'd debated waking him, but after everything we'd done, he had needed to rest. Since he was a shifter, his ass would heal quickly, but he needed rest for that healing to take place.

And I had to admit, it was easier to make my exit while he slept because I hadn't wanted to say goodbye. I'd found a notepad and pen on the hotel desk and managed to compose a note after two false starts. It wasn't like me to overthink things like that, but I wanted everything I did for Storm to be perfect.

My wolf had urged me to stay, but I'd needed to get back to my friend's house and change before my interview. Walking away from Storm had been physically painful, but I didn't want to think too hard about what that meant because I needed to focus on making a good impression for my first day. I'd been hired with a one-month probationary period, and I intended to wow my employers. I'd trained for years to learn single-minded focus, and I couldn't remember the last time it had been this hard to achieve. But if I could ignore what was going on around me in a war zone, surely I could stop thinking about how badly I wanted to bury myself in Storm again and just do my fucking job.

I finished trimming my beard and checked my appearance in the mirror one last time. Clean. Neat. Well put-together.

The drive to the Howlers' estate took about thirty minutes in traffic. Hopefully I'd be able to find some place closer, but from the search I'd done the night before, anything closer was going to be way out of my price range. The salary they offered me was quite generous, so while I might have to live further out to start with, I'd be able to build up some savings, assuming I liked the job and they were satisfied with my performance. They would be because I was damn good at keeping people safe.

The Howlers' butler, Arthur, let me in and showed me to King's office. When I stepped inside, I froze.

Storm was there.

His eyes widened when I came in, and even though he'd schooled his face quickly, King had noticed. "Do you two know each other?"

My mind spun trying to figure out what was going on, but I kept my face impassive. I wouldn't reveal anything about what had happened between me and Storm, especially considering I was now fairly certain Storm was one of the Howler brothers I hadn't met. I'd been trying so hard to keep from thinking about him during my interview, and their resemblance wasn't particularly noticeable. Seeing Storm and King side by side, though, I could tell they had the same eyes and the same shape to their mouths, even if otherwise, Storm was soft where King was hard lines of determination.

If Storm was related to King and Garrett, one of the other brothers I'd met, no wonder he felt smothered by them. A few seconds with King and I'd pegged him as a control freak. I could easily imagine him thinking it was his job to keep Storm safe.

"We met when Jax visited Tooth and Claw the other night," Storm said, looking right at me and smiling. I could feel his smile as if he were running his hands over me. It looked like this job wasn't going to work out after all. I couldn't work for his family and sleep with him, but I wasn't sure I could resist the temptation of him if I saw him day after day.

"You met him?" King asked, a hard edge to his voice. He knew Storm had spent the night with someone, and it wasn't going to be hard to figure out that someone was me.

"Yes," Storm said, refusing to give an inch. Watching him stand up to his brother was hot as hell. If I stayed here, I'd constantly be fighting to keep from walking around with a hard-on.

"I'm sorry. I don't think this is going to work out. I hadn't realized I'd be working for someone I know. I appreciate your consideration, but—"

"Wait," Storm said, frowning at me. "There's no reason for you to—"

"Just how well do you know Jax?" King asked, his voice eerily soft now. I could sense his wolf, and that made my own wolf prepare for battle. *Protect*, he insisted.

But Storm didn't need protection. He wasn't in danger from his brothers. They might be irritating, but that was because they cared for him, and me getting into a fight with King would ruin any chance we had of seeing each other again.

King glanced toward me and growled. I prayed he wouldn't start anything. I would defend myself, and as powerful as he looked, I was sure I could take him, but if more of his brothers joined in, I wouldn't be able to come out on top without injuring them seriously. Storm wouldn't thank me for harming his brothers, no matter how pissed off he was.

"Back off, King. I want to speak to Jax alone."

King shook his head. "Not until I have an explanation of—"

"Later," Storm said.

King didn't move, but Storm's expression softened. "Please just let me handle this."

King sighed, obviously more easily swayed by Storm's imploring look than his annoyance. "I'll give you a few minutes, but that's all."

After the door closed behind him, Storm looked back at me. "Hi."

"Tell me you didn't know I was interviewing with your brothers?" I hated to think he'd deceived me, but—

"No. I never would have done that. I knew someone was interviewing today for a bodyguard position, but I had no idea it was you. When I met you at Tooth and Claw, you were just a hot-as-fuck stranger."

I couldn't help but smile at that. "I didn't know either. I wouldn't have left the club with you if I did, and now—"

"We can work with this."

I frowned. "What do you mean?"

"King thinks you're perfect for watching me when I want to break away from them. I can pretend I'm going out, but I'll really be with you."

That was so tempting, but sleeping with an employer wasn't right. Even if I would cross that line, King had made it very clear that relationships between the guards and the people we were protecting was forbidden and would result in immediate termination. "I can't be your bodyguard and…"

"Sleep with me?"

"Among other things."

Storm raised his brows. "Are you saying you'd rather guard me on my way to be with someone else?"

I growled. *Mine.* The thought of Storm with someone else had my claws trying to extend and my fangs descending. I squeezed my eyes shut and took a few calming breaths. How did this man have me so off balance?

"I take it that's a no," Storm said.

"The easiest way to solve this is for me to resign."

"And then leave town and never see me again."

The idea of that sent pain knifing through my chest. My wolf howled. *Stay.* But how could I? "Storm, I—"

"You're not going to resign. You're exactly the sort of person we need working here. Someone we can trust. Someone strong but kind. We've been looking for the right person for a while. Even Shadow likes you, and he's skittish around most people."

I wondered what had happened to the youngest of the Howlers, but I wasn't going to ask, especially not now.

"I'm glad I was able to make him comfortable. My unit did a lot of rescues, and I had to learn how to get terrified people to trust me quickly if I was going to get them to safety."

Storm laid a hand on my arm. "I would trust you to do anything."

He had. Without even knowing me, Storm had trusted me with his body, trusted me to hurt him just as much as he wanted to be hurt, and dear Goddess, I wanted to do it again.

That couldn't happen if I stayed, but if I left, who would protect him? Someone with far less skill than me. Someone who wouldn't value his safety like I did. King had explained that their family had plenty of enemies, and the lion shifters were scheming against them. They wanted to take control of the shifter council King headed, which was composed of the leaders of the most powerful shifter groups in the city. They controlled the local black market, but King was working to bring them more legitimacy and move away from criminal activities that harmed others, no matter how lucrative they might be.

What if the lions came after Storm, and I wasn't here for him?

My wolf snarled inside me, desperate to convince me to stay. *Protect. Mate.*

Was my wolf right? Was Storm my mate? If so, how could I leave him? But if I stayed, I'd have to keep my hands off him because if we were caught together, I'd be sent away.

Storm moved until he was standing right in front of me. Then he took my hands in his. "Please stay."

I couldn't deny him. "I will, but if I do, we can't... I can't sleep with you again."

Even as I said that, I saw the heat in his eyes, and my body responded to it. Denying myself—denying us both—was going to be the hardest thing I'd ever done.

He let me go and stepped away. "As long as you're here, we can take things slowly and see what we can work out."

I frowned. "There's no working things out if I'm employed by your family."

"Then I guess I'll have to be sure you're not the one who accompanies me the next time I leave Tooth and Claw with—"

"No," I growled. I gripped his wrist, squeezing until he gasped. I knew it was wrong to tell him we couldn't be together and also prevent him from being with anyone else, but my wolf didn't believe in fairness.

"Your wolf doesn't like that idea," Storm gave me a wicked smile.

"He doesn't, but he's not controlling things."

"No, you are. And I'll let you. I'll let you control this if you promise to stay."

I narrowed my eyes, sensing a trap. "You'll let me control what, exactly?"

"Us. I'll let you decide when you're going to give in to what's between us. I know you feel it too, but I'll submit to what you want."

"I will not risk being caught by your brothers because then I can't be the one who protects you."

"And you're the best?"

"Damn right."

Take. Claim. My wolf insisted, but I couldn't go down that path. I also couldn't walk away. "I'm staying, and I'm holding you to your promise to let me be in charge."

Storm smiled. "I promise to do as you say. May I call King in now so he can rant a bit and then tell you your responsibilities for the rest of the day?"

"Are you going to tell him exactly how well you know me?"

"Later, yes. But don't worry. Your job is safe. King is stubborn and difficult, and he wants to control everything I do, but I've learned how to sway him when I really need to."

I had no doubt that was true.

7

STORM

The last few weeks had been hell. I'd confessed to King that Jax was the man I'd been with the night I'd "disappeared." Predictably, he'd snarled and ranted. He'd threatened to kill Jax and then to fire him, but eventually, he'd admitted—more or less—that he was being an asshole. I'd chosen to be with Jax without any coercion whatsoever, and Jax was perfect for the job.

King had told Garrett, and I'd gone through the whole thing again, although with less claws, fangs, and posturing, and more cold logic. But dealing with my stubborn, arrogant brothers was easy compared to what had been going on since then. I'd told Jax I would let him have control, but that didn't mean I wasn't planning to tempt him. I wouldn't ask him directly or force his hand, but I never said I didn't know how to be a bit of a brat.

One morning, I pulled on a pair of tiny green running shorts. They looked like they were at least a size too small, and the color made my eyes appear bright green instead of their usual hazel. I messed with my curls until they looked as soft and inviting as I wanted them to. Then, wearing nothing else but my running shoes, I sought out Jax to let him know he needed to accompany me on an early morning run.

I saw the muscles in his throat flex as he swallowed hard when I approached him. His eyes were dark with heat, but all he said was, "Yes, sir."

He jogged a few feet behind me, never breathing hard during the ten-mile run through the trails that led into the forest. I glanced over my shoulder numerous times, but he never met my gaze. When we got back to the house, he said, "Will there be anything else?"

I wanted to grab him and shake him. I knew what he was feeling. How could he act so distant?"

"No, but you shouldn't go in without stretching."

He sighed, but he didn't contradict me. I angled myself perfectly, bending over so my ass was on display, sitting down and opening my legs wide, then oh so slowly sliding forward until my torso lay against the ground. When I sat back up, I caught him staring.

"I never miss a chance to stretch. I wouldn't want to lose any of this flexibility."

He coughed and looked at his watch. "I think I'm supposed to... um..."

I'd gotten a reaction, so I took pity on him. "Go on. I'm headed in."

I'd thought I had things moving in the right direction, but the more I tempted him, the more stoic he became. I decided to try seducing him with food.

A few days after I had taken Jax on the run, he accompanied me to visit one of our suppliers, a tiger who could be rather temperamental. When we returned home, I motioned for Jax to follow me to the kitchen.

"Mara, our cook, made brownies today. She used to make two pans, one with icing and one with caramel drizzle, but we all eat them so fast she had to start making two pans of each. I could eat a whole pan of them myself easily."

He frowned. "I probably shouldn't—"

"Yes, you should." I took his arm, intending to pull him there, but the shock of the contact froze me in place. We stared at each other until I let go and stepped back. "I'd really like you to try them."

"Then I will."

I felt slightly steadier when we reached the kitchen. Jax had felt the jolt that ran between us. It had startled him as much as it had me. That was a good sign, right?

Mara had texted me a few moments before to let me know the brownies were ready, but someone—my bet would be on Bryce—had already been into them. Fortunately, there were plenty left. I cut us several of each. "Let's take them to the library," I suggested. It would be quiet there, so we were more likely to have a chance to talk than here in the kitchen.

Jax eyed me warily. "Just while we eat?"

For as long as I can get you to stay. "Yes. I can pour us some coffee too."

"I'll get the coffee. You like cream and sugar, right?"

"How did you know?"

"I've been watching you for weeks, Storm."

Watching me, learning my habits. Obsessing over me, like I had over him?

I pulled out a tray and set the brownies on it. Jax added the mugs, and I started to lift it, but Jax took it from me. "You don't have to do everything, Storm. I've got this."

Warmth spread through my chest. I liked serving people, helping them, but I also liked when Jax did that for me. I knew all the reasons why spending time with him was a bad idea. I didn't want to have to argue with King about my relationship with Jax. I certainly didn't want Jax to leave, and I doubted a few minutes together enjoying some brownies would really change anything. It would only make me long for him more when he went back to ignoring me, but that didn't mean I was going to give up this chance to be with him.

Jax followed me to the library. I closed the door behind us and gestured toward the table and chairs in the alcove created by a bay window.

"This is a beautiful room," Jax said.

"It's my favorite place in the house. I probably spent more hours of my childhood here than anywhere, except maybe the woods.

"Did you read a lot?"

"Yes, I still do."

Jax put the tray on the table, and we each settled into one of the chairs.

He was practically drooling as he studied the plate of brownies. Asking Mara to make them had been a great idea.

"Which one should I try first?" he asked.

"It's hard to say. Are you a caramel fan? Bryce would devour anything if you put caramel on it. I've seen him eat a whole pan of these seconds after they came out of the oven. He just stood at the counter and shoved them in his mouth. But while I think they are exquisite, I like the iced ones best."

Jax reached for one of the ones with icing. When he bit into it, he groaned, and my cock responded to the sound. Once he swallowed, he said, "This is the best brownie I've ever tasted."

"I told you. Mara is amazing."

"Everything I've eaten here has been fantastic, but these…"

"Try a caramel one."

Jax did, and the look on his face as he tasted it was so

much like the way he'd watched me as he'd fucked into me, filling me up, that my cock grew fully hard. Watching him eat brownies should not be so hot, but I'd known it would be because I'd remembered the ecstasy on his face when he'd eaten the chocolate cake at the hotel. "Do you love everything chocolate?"

"It's one of my weaknesses."

"As far as I can tell, it's your only weakness." I barely managed not to run my hand over his biceps. Goddess, his arms were gorgeous.

He snorted. "Hardly, you are my—"

My heart sang. I was one of his weaknesses.

Jax shook his head. "I didn't mean—"

"You've done a much better job staying away from me than you have with these brownies."

"The consequences are different. A plate of brownies means a little bit of extra time at the gym. But being with you is…"

There was so much I wanted to say, but this wasn't how I wanted our time together to go.

We ate our brownies in silence for several moments. Then, needing to get us back on track, I said, "Do you read much?"

"I do, actually. We had terrible internet access where I was last stationed, so reading was one of the few entertainments we had. We'd get boxes of books from the States, but we couldn't be choosy."

"What was your favorite book that you read there?"

Before answering, Jax reached out and rubbed his thumb across my cheek close to the corner of my mouth. I held my breath as his touch sent heat through me. I wanted to turn into his touch, grab his wrist, and suck his thumb into my mouth.

"You… um… you had icing on your face, and I…"

"Thank you," I said, my voice shaky.

We stared at each other for a few seconds, but he didn't kiss me like I'd hoped.

"Your… um… your favorite book?"

"Oh, right. You're probably going to laugh, but—"

"No, I would never laugh at you for what you like."

His eyes widened slightly, and I was sure he was thinking of how he'd told me he'd never mock me for my desires, just like I was.

He cleared his throat and continued. "One box contained a wolf shifter romance series. I was the last one to pick that day, and it was all that was left. I read the first one, and wow, it was filthy, but also so good. I flew through the series and then read them again. I re-read them last week."

"What's it called?"

Color bloomed across his cheeks, and it made him even sexier. I wanted to kiss him so badly.

"The series is called Wolves of Arundel, but—"

"I love that series. It's so hot."

"You've read it?"

"Tons of times. I've got it here." I walked over to one of the bookshelves and crouched down so I could open the doors of the cabinet at the bottom. I had to lift a few stacks of paperbacks out of the way, but I found the right ones fairly quickly. I pulled out all five books and brought them back to the table. "See, here they are."

Jax picked one up and turned it over in his hands. "When I read this, it was the first time I realized I might enjoy spanking a man."

We had to be fated for each other. "Same for me. I mean, I was thinking of being spanked."

Jax stared at me, eyes filled with heat. I held still, not daring to break the silence, but after a few seconds, he turned away and picked up his coffee mug. When he'd had a few sips, he said, "If these are some of your favorites, why are they hidden away in a cabinet instead of on the shelf?"

"You know how you thought I might laugh at you for reading them?"

He nodded.

"I thought my older brothers would laugh, so I hid them."

"That doesn't sound like you."

Jax was right. Even if they did laugh, this was my home. I had just as much right as any of my siblings to put my books —no matter the genre—on the shelf. I scooped up the books, walked over to a shelf that had a few wolf statues on it, moved one, and set up the series in its place. "There."

"Much better," he said.

I started to reach for another brownie and realized they were all gone. Jax winced. "I didn't mean to eat that many, but they are just—"

"That good. It's possible there are still some left if all my brothers haven't found out about them."

"Do you want me to get you another one?"

"No, I'm fine." As good as the brownies were, being with Jax and sharing things we were interested in was much better. I felt more settled inside than I had since the night we'd spent together.

Silence stretched between us for a moment, and I was afraid Jax would insist that he needed to go, so I asked the first question that came to mind. "What are you doing tomorrow? You have the day off, right?"

"I do. Denny asked if I want to go see a movie with him, so I might do that."

"You should. I really like Denny." And he's straight, so I knew there was nothing there but friendship.

"Me too. He's fun to work with."

"So what's your all-time favorite movie?"

"All-time favorite, hmm?"

"Yes, and no cheating and listing like ten."

He tilted his head as he thought, and I was happy to just stare at him. "*Return of the Jedi.*"

I could so see that. "Yeah. That fits."

He rolled his eyes. "I'm glad you approve. What about you?"

"*Lady and the Tramp.*"

A laugh burst from him. "Really?"

"Yes. I was probably three years old when I saw it for the first time. I absolutely loved it, and that's never changed. I've seen it more than any other movie. I even dressed up like Tramp for Halloween one year. My brothers thought it was the funniest thing ever, a wolf dressing up as a dog."

Jax grinned. "It is a little bit ridiculous, but I bet you were adorable. I wish I could've seen you."

"I've got a picture somewhere. Most of our family albums are in here."

"Oh, wow. I would love to see some of those."

I was about to seriously embarrass myself and probably my brothers, but if showing Jax pictures of us as kids would keep him here with me, I didn't mind at all.

This time when I crossed the room, Jax stood and followed me. I opened the cabinet beneath one of the other shelves and read through the labels on the photo albums inside. I'd put a lot of them together myself. After my mother had died, my father hadn't cared about all the boxes of pictures she'd saved. King and Lacey had made sure they were safe, but they had never taken the time to put them in albums, so once I was old enough, I took care of it.

Jax and I sat down on the floor right by the cabinet, and I

flipped through an album until I found the picture I was looking for. "Here I am."

Jax ran a hand over the cellophane covering the picture. "Wow. You were even more adorable than I'd guessed." I glanced up at him, and we both cracked up. I was wearing a brown sweat suit, a headband with pointy ears, and you could see the tail that had been pinned to my butt. I looked ridiculous. Lacey had even painted whiskers on my face and colored the tip of my nose black.

"You could have just gone in wolf form," Jax said.

"No way. I couldn't say trick-or-treat then." That set us off into another fit of laughter.

When we calmed down, he pointed to a figure beside me. "Is that Bryce?"

"Yes." He'd dressed up as a football player. I wasn't sure where we'd found a helmet small enough, since he must have only been six.

Jax moved closer to me as I showed him more of my favorite pictures from the collection of albums. Our legs were pressed together, and the heat of him was making it hard for me to concentrate.

I found my favorite picture of King. It was from the eighties. He and Lacey were wearing leg warmers and headbands, and she'd been trying to teach him a dance she'd made up. Jax and I were laughing like hyenas over it when the library door burst open.

"Storm, are you—oh, hello, Jax." It was Bryce.

Jax stood abruptly. "Storm was showing me some photos. But I should probably go now."

"No need," Bryce said. "King just wanted me to track Storm down and tell him King needs to talk to him as soon as he's available."

I groaned. "What does he want now?"

Bryce shrugged. "I don't know. He just said you weren't answering his texts and told me to find you." My phone was on silent, and I hadn't been paying attention to it while I was with Jax.

"Fine. I'll go see him in a little while."

"Good luck with that."

Bryce left then, and I turned to Jax. "King can wait."

"No, this was… I shouldn't be here with you."

Anger surged through me. "This was a fucking nice way to spend the afternoon, and you know it."

Jax closed his eyes and pressed his lips together. "You're right. It has been. I'm sorry, but you should go see your brother now."

Damn King for fucking this up.

"I have to take the tray back and—"

Jax was already putting the albums back in the cabinet, taking care to stack them in order. "I'll take care of everything."

If only he really could.

Nothing I did after that—having him come to my office at Tooth and Claw to consult on a security matter and then walking through the public playroom on our way out, wearing the sluttiest outfit I owned, posing whenever he entered the room—tempted him the way our time in the library had. He'd treated me with impassive professionalism, and I hated it. I hated King for it. I knew Jax was doing the right thing in his mind. The man was a pillar of integrity, but this whole situation was fucking stupid. Every day, I became more convinced that we were mates, because if we weren't, it wouldn't be so fucking painful to be ignored by him.

Would being ignored be as hard for Jax to take? What else could I do but force myself to be just as professional and distant as Jax? It didn't help. Jax remained as stoic as ever. If

I hadn't occasionally seen heat in his gaze when he looked at me, I might have decided he truly didn't want me anymore.

Despite how hard it was to be close to him and unable to touch him like I wanted to, I still loved that he was always nearby, making sure no one even looked at me in a way that was suspicious. I could feel his need to protect me like a warm blanket. If only that was enough.

Weeks passed, and I'd begun to wonder how much longer I could go on like this without breaking and begging him to fuck me again. Then everything changed because King found his mate—his very vulnerable *human* mate. As usual, King decided to be a stubborn ass about the situation, and Jax was the only one I trusted to give me the help I needed.

Once I had King's mate, Emerson, settled in our guest-house, I sought out Jax. According to our butler, Arthur, who knew everything that went on in our household, Jax had worked an overnight shift because one of the perimeter guards had called in sick. He'd crashed in one of the guest rooms rather than driving home and was likely still there.

I wondered if I would have to wake him up. As thrilling as the thought of him all sleep-tousled and still warm from bed was, seeing him like that would make it impossible for me to focus on what I needed from him. But when I knocked on his door, he responded immediately.

My heart pounded as I heard his footsteps approach. When he opened the door, his eyes widened. He obviously hadn't expected it to be me. I wanted to explain, to tell him why I was there, but all I could do was stare. He was shirtless, his chest hair curled and damp like he'd just been in the shower. I wanted to lick the water droplets off him, suck on his puckered nipples—

"Storm?"

I forced my gaze upward to meet his. "Sorry. I…"

"I assume you're here for a reason."

Please let him listen to me. "I need to ask you a favor. Can I come in?" He glanced back into the room before looking at me again. I held up my hands. "I'm just here to talk. I promise. This is serious, or I wouldn't have bothered you."

"Are you okay?" The concern in his eyes warmed me.

"I am. It has to do with King."

He opened the door wider and gestured for me to come in. The room was perfectly clean and neat. There were no shoes or clothes on the floor, nothing at all besides one duffel bag, and it was zipped shut. The bed was neatly made, as if he'd never slept in it.

Jax sat on the edge of the bed. I wanted to join him there, but he gestured to the single chair by the window. "You can have the chair unless you prefer to stand."

I preferred to push him back onto the mattress and forget about King and Emerson and the escalating dangers we faced from the Crown family. I'd straddle Jax, shove his sweats down his legs, and take him inside me. But that wasn't going to happen.

I sank into the chair and forced myself not to fidget. "There was an incident at Tooth and Claw tonight. A human managed to get in, and a group of lion shifters, including a few of the Crown brothers, attempted to lure him away with them. Emerson, the young human, was drunk, so he was particularly vulnerable, and they knew it. King rescued Emerson, and he and King reacted to each other very strongly."

"What was a human doing at Tooth and Claw?"

The club was supposed to be for shifters only. Occasionally, humans tried to sneak in, seeking a thrill, but they were usually stopped before they got through the door. "We're still looking into how he managed to sneak in. Obviously, we need to tighten security, but his safety was our first concern. He doesn't have anywhere to go, so I've put him in the guesthouse."

"He's staying here?"

I sighed and pushed my hand through my hair. "I brought him back here late last night. King went to see him a little while ago, and he reacted so intensely that he nearly shifted in front of Emerson and had to go for a run in the woods. Based on what I've seen and what Emerson told me, I'm nearly certain they're fated mates."

Jax's eyes went wide. "Wow. That's… wow."

"Yeah. It is. And Emerson has nowhere to go. His ex-boyfriend kicked him out, and that's what led to him showing up trashed at a shifter club. King told me to escort him home, but since he doesn't have a home right now, and King isn't thinking clearly, I'm keeping Emerson here. The Crown brothers saw how protective King was of him, and they won't hesitate to strike at King by hurting him."

"No, they won't," Jax agreed. "We have to protect him."

I loved that he said "we." I knew he meant my family and the other guards who worked for us, but it felt good that in only a few months, he'd become part of our extended family. Our instincts had been right. He was exactly the kind of guard we had been looking for.

"I need you to watch the guesthouse, and if Emerson needs to leave, I want you to accompany him anywhere he wants to go. Get Denny to be your driver. Since he's young and easygoing, he won't be intimidating to Emerson."

"And what about me?"

"You've already told me you're good with frightened humans. You're the only one I trust to do this." I didn't miss the way Jax's breath hitched when I said that. "I know I'm asking a lot because it goes directly against what King told me to do, but I promise I'll take the blame for everything. King won't be angry with you for following my orders."

"I'm not worried about that. You know I'd do anything for you."

"Would you?"

He held my gaze, and tension crackled between us. He knew exactly what I wanted him to do, but he'd told me no. I could feel his wolf pushing at him, though, trying to goad him into doing exactly what I wanted. Relief coursed through me at the sensation. Nothing had changed since the night we were together. Jax still wanted me just as much as I wanted him. He was just really damn good at denying himself. I had to prioritize Emerson's safety, but later, when things settled down, I was going to push Jax until he gave us both what we longed for.

8

JAX

A s I stood guard in front of the Howlers' guesthouse, all I could think about was how good it had been to talk to Storm.

I'd seen him every day for the past few months, but other than exchanging brief words while I was on duty, we hadn't really talked to each other in weeks. I'd forced myself to practically ignore him, especially after he kept pulling stunts like running in microscopic shorts and taunting me by leading me through the playroom at Tooth and Claw. It was torture having him there in my bedroom just a few feet away, knowing that if I made even the tiniest move, he'd respond the way he had the one night we'd spent with each other. Not touching him was killing me, but treating him like he was a stranger was even worse.

I'd done my best to appear impartial to him, but every time I was assigned to guard him, I rushed home after my shift and jerked off to every filthy fantasy I could conjure up involving Storm on his knees, taking my commands, opening himself up to me utterly. How much longer could I go without having him again?

At least these new developments with a human staying on the Howler property and the potential of an increased threat from the Crowns would give me something to focus on, though they would also force me to talk to Storm more. I'd already had to call him to find out if it was okay to take Emerson to Tooth and Claw to meet with King. Storm believed King needed to be confronted by Emerson, so he'd said yes and once again promised to take the blame. I was still set to face King's wrath when we arrived because I sure as hell wasn't going to allow it to be directed at Emerson.

I liked the young man. Despite him being human, he showed no fear of me or Denny, and he was obviously ready to stand up to King, something plenty of shifters were afraid to do. While Denny drove us to Tooth and Claw, Emerson pumped us for information about the Howler family. He especially wanted to know why King and Storm insisted he was in danger, but it wasn't my place to give him answers King didn't want him to have. If Storm wanted to tell him more, that was fine, but he wasn't going to hear gossip from me, so I kept my answers vague. "In my line of work, I've learned to assume there's always danger lurking everywhere."

Denny huffed out a laugh. "Always a pessimist."

"A pessimist is never disappointed." When I'd been in the military, I'd learned to expect everything to go ass up. I had contingency plans for my contingency plans.

Denny rolled his eyes. "That came straight from Garrett, didn't it?"

"Possibly." The wording had, but not the sentiment. Most of the Howler staff saw Garrett as cold and calculating, but I recognized in him the same need to be prepared that I had. Staying distant was how Garrett dealt with the need to be constantly on guard, alert for threats or danger. He'd apparently developed that because of a hellish childhood, whereas I'd learned it in a combat zone.

"Garrett's one of King's brothers, right?" Emerson asked.

Denny glanced back at Emerson as he came to a stop at a red light. "You haven't met all of King's brothers?"

"I've only met Storm."

Denny grinned. "He's the most personable."

Just the mention of his name sent heat through me. I covered my reaction by scolding Denny. "If you want to keep this job, you've got to learn to say less."

He rolled his eyes, not the least bit chastised. "You like Storm."

So goddamned much. I knew Storm had told his brothers that he and I had been together, but I wasn't sure who among the staff knew. Denny didn't seem to be teasing me though. He was too open and earnest for that, but I needed to keep this conversation professional. "He is easier to talk to than some of the others." That was as much as I would admit to.

When we pulled up at Tooth and Claw, Emerson insisted he could drive himself home, since he'd left his car there, but I wasn't leaving him. If King refused to let him stay, Denny would be driving him home. Storm was trusting me to keep him safe, and that's what I would do.

"So King doesn't know I'm here?" Emerson asked.

"Right." I pulled out a key to the employees only entrance to the club. "Storm thought that was best. King is in his office. Take this and head on inside."

He stared at the key like he was confused. "You're giving me a key to the club?"

"Storm is giving you a key to the club," Denny said. "It would be best to leave us out of it."

My wolf urged me to protect Storm by taking the blame, but I kept my mouth shut. King might be annoyed, but he would never take his anger out on his younger brother. He wanted to protect Storm as much as I did.

I could tell Emerson wanted to question us more, but he also wanted to get to King, so he didn't try too hard. Once he was inside, Denny and I got back in the car to wait.

"What's up with you?" Denny asked.

"What do you mean?"

"You're always more of a stickler for the rules than I am, but you're really being a hard ass today."

Shit. I'd hoped my frustration wasn't showing. "I'm not going to gossip about the Howlers with someone who's just met them, especially someone they haven't even vetted yet."

Denny snorted. "He's a human. How much of a threat can he be?"

"If he's working with other shifters, he could be a lethal one."

"Do you really always see the worst in everyone?"

I'd been looking for trouble for so long, I didn't have a choice anymore. "I always think through the worst-case scenario. I wouldn't be standing here now if I didn't."

"I get that," Denny said. "You've dealt with a lot of life-and-death situations."

"I have. I know most things aren't that serious, but I'd rather assume the worst and have things work out better than the other way around."

Denny gave me a worried frown. "You need to relax occasionally. Have you even been out since you started this job?"

I had no interest in going out with anyone but Storm, and I couldn't risk that. If Emerson and King were mates, Storm was right. Emerson would be a target, but an attack on him could be an attack on the entire family. Storm was vulnerable, and he needed me. I couldn't do anything that might prevent me from watching him as closely as I needed to.

"Is something up with you and Storm?"

Shit. I needed to remember that Denny was a lot more perceptive than his easygoing manner suggested. "What do you mean?"

"I may not be bodyguard material, but I notice a lot driving people around all day. You tense up every time his name is mentioned, and I hardly think admitting he's the easiest Howler brother to talk to is major gossip."

"Bryce is perfectly personable."

Denny snorted. "He can be when he's in the mood, but he's not a people pleaser like Storm."

"Storm isn't a pushover though. People think—" Denny's eyes widened, and I stopped. I was totally giving myself away.

"That was rather... defensive," Denny said with a smirk. "I know you've been assigned to watch over Storm plenty of times, but I didn't realize you'd gotten to know him that well."

"I haven't. I don't know why I said that."

He laid a hand on my arm. "The rumors are true, aren't they?"

Oh fuck. "What rumors?"

"That you and Storm had a thing before you took the job."

I glared at Denny, and he raised his hands in a surrendering gesture. "You probably think I love to gossip, but I mostly listen. If you need to talk, I swear I would never repeat anything you told me. I haven't repeated those rumors either. I've only heard them."

I sighed. I didn't think Denny was going to say anything,

but I didn't like thinking everyone in the household knew. "I'd really hoped that knowledge had stayed with the family."

"In a household as close as this one, there are very few secrets."

"Which likely means rumors don't stay in the family either, so it won't be any time at all before the lions know about Emerson."

Denny nodded. "That's probably true. But we'll deal with that as it comes. Right now, we can deal with you."

I bit back a snarl. "I'm just fine."

"Which is why you're fidgeting when usually you sit so still I have to check and make sure you're still breathing?"

I growled. "There's nothing anyone can do to help. The rumors are true. Before Storm knew I'd be working for his family, we were together briefly, but we're not now, and we won't be. Storm is one of my employers. I'm here to keep him safe, and that's all."

"But that's not what either one of you wants."

"It doesn't matter what I want. It's part of my contract that I keep my hands off the people I guard."

Denny frowned. "Have you considered that maybe there's more here than simple attraction. I've seen him watching you, and nothing ruffles you other than talking about him, so—"

"We're done discussing this." Denny looked hurt, and I immediately regretted snapping at him. "I'm sorry. It's just... I don't want to talk about it anymore because it's not a possibility. I need to stay focused on my job."

"If you can't be with Storm, then get back out there and find somebody else."

My wolf growled, angry at the thought of me touching anyone but Storm. "I'm better off on my own right now."

Denny raised his brows. "Are you?"

"Don't push your luck."

"I thought you knew by now that I usually do."

I sighed. "Are you ever serious?"

"I'm serious right now when I say that if you change your mind and you want to talk more, I'm here."

I really did like Denny. If I was going to confide in someone, he'd be on my list, but I couldn't even let myself think about being Storm's mate. "Thanks. I'll keep that in mind."

We stayed quiet for a while, but as much as I tried not to think about Storm, he was the only thing on my mind. I continued to replay the conversation we'd had before he sent me to guard Emerson. I'd told him I would do anything for him, and he'd questioned me because the "anything" he wanted was the one thing I couldn't do. He wanted me to take him again, to dominate him, to remind him he wasn't fragile and didn't always need protection. But while his body could take plenty of damage, and he had every right to choose who he wanted to be with and when, he *did* need protection against ruthless lion shifters and the other enemies his family had made. He was strong and capable, but against the weapons they would use, he was helpless. I needed to be here to save him, which meant I had to hold back the one thing we both wanted: another night together.

9

STORM

Ever since I'd gone to see Jax the day before, he was all I could think about. It was as if actually talking to him had broken through all the barriers I'd tried to erect. Not that I'd done a good job with walling up my feelings, but now I felt like I was going to come out of my skin. I hadn't slept the night before. I'd paced my room, then eventually gone out to the woods to run in wolf form. But even as my paws pounded the leaf litter on the forest floor, all I thought about was Jax. I needed him. I couldn't take this anymore. I wasn't going to let the rules my brothers had set keep me from him any longer. I would do whatever was necessary to change their minds. There was no reason Jax couldn't be my Dom and still protect me.

I had work to do at the club until late in the evening. When I got home, I almost went straight to the guesthouse looking for Jax, but I told myself to go to my room first to shower, change, and consider my strategy.

It would be even better if I slept some before I talked to him, but as soon as I got to my room, I went to the window that looked out across the lawn toward the guesthouse. When

I let my eyes shift to my lupine, I could make out Jax's figure standing on the porch.

Need. Want. Go to him, my wolf urged, squirming inside me, wanting to find his way out. If I let him, he'd race to Jax as fast as he could. I seriously considered doing just that. If I visited him in wolf form, he wouldn't send me away, but that wasn't what I wanted. I wanted his hands on me as a human, and I couldn't wait any longer.

Going to him was reckless and foolish, and against his wishes, but there was such a driving need inside me that I couldn't stop myself. I took the stairs several at a time, then gripped the post at the bottom to whirl myself around so I was headed toward the back door. I nearly crashed into Bryce as he came down the hall.

"Where you going?"

"To do something foolish. And you are not going to stop me."

"Storm, if you're going out, take Jax with you. He can call someone else to watch the guesthouse."

"I promise if I leave, I'll go with Jax." That promise was safe to make.

"Storm, are you—"

"Just let me do this. Let me make my own choices."

"Is this about Jax?"

"Promise you won't say anything to the rest of them, please."

Bryce frowned. "I was always the one you trusted with your secrets when we were little."

"Because Lacey and King were always trying to stop me from doing anything fun."

"Your idea of fun was also usually dangerous."

I shoved at his shoulder. "So was yours."

"That's why we made good confidants."

"I'm going to convince Jax that staying apart is making us both miserable, but please don't tell anyone."

"Who would I tell anyway? King's busy trying to convince himself he can stay away from his mate. Garrett's gone as usual, and Shadow is off playing in the woods. No one is here for me to tell."

"You could tell them later."

Bryce shook his head. "As long as you're not in danger, what you do should be your business. All I want is to keep you safe."

"I have Jax for that."

"I'm glad for that. Go on." He gestured toward the back door. "I won't tell."

I raced through the kitchen and burst out of the house.

Need. Now.

I know, I told my wolf. *I'm going to get him back for us.*

I had to force myself to slow down as I approached the guesthouse, but even so, Jax looked alarmed when he saw me.

"Is something wrong?"

"No, I just needed to see you."

He frowned. "You could've called with anything you needed to say."

"It's not so much what I want to say as what I want to do."

He held up his hands. "Storm, I—"

"Jax, I can't stop myself anymore. I know why you want to keep your distance, but are you really able to shut down the connection between us? Because I can't. I tried, but it never really worked, and as soon as I talked to you again, my need for you came back stronger than ever. I think about you all the time."

Jax looked like he was in pain. "I think about you all the

89

time too, but we can't be together because at best, King will fire me and prevent me from getting another job in town. At worst, I'll have to fight him. I don't want to hurt your brother."

He mentioned fighting King so casually. Most people, even the other guards, were terrified of him. "You think you could take him?"

"I know I could."

No hesitation. "Fuck, that's hot."

He frowned at me. "Beating up your brother is not hot."

"The fact that you're strong enough to is. My whole life, he's been my fiercest protector and now—"

"That's me."

I took his hand and tugged, trying to lead him away from the house.

"Where are we going? I need to stay here to keep watch over Emerson."

"We have the perimeter guards to alert us if anything is happening further away, and we'll hear Emerson if he tries to leave. Has King come to see him?"

Jax sighed. "Yes, and a few minutes after he went inside, he burst through the door like he couldn't get away fast enough. I heard Emerson crying. He sounded devastated."

Why was my brother such an idiot? "I guess I should go see if I can talk some sense into him later."

"He's in the rose garden. I called one of the other guards, and they found him."

At least King was still on the property. He often went to the rose garden when he needed to think. When my mother was alive, it was her thinking spot too. King felt close to her there.

I moved closer to Jax and reached up to cup his face. "I

know this is complicated, but right now, I just need you to kiss me."

I thought he'd deny me or at least protest more, but he pulled me to him and kissed me like he was dying and my lips were the only thing that could save him.

I slid my fingers into his hair and sank against him, pressing our bodies together. It felt so right to be in his arms again. I hadn't even realized how empty I'd been feeling without that buzz of sensation he created in me.

"Need you," he murmured when he pulled back for air.

"I know." I sank to my knees, longing to serve him. As I reached for the fastenings of his pants, I almost begged him to order me to suck him off, but I was too afraid he'd refuse. I just started to slide his zipper down when the guesthouse door creaked.

Fuck. I scrambled to my feet, almost tumbling over in my haste. The second Jax had his pants buttoned, he rushed toward the front of the house.

"Did you need something, Emerson?" I'd moved close enough to hear him easily, but stayed out of sight.

"I need to find King."

"It's better for you to stay here."

Emerson made a frustrated sound. If he'd been a wolf, it would have been a growl. "Let me be more clear. I am going to find King."

I smoothed down my ruffled clothes and stepped out from my hiding place. "King is in the rose garden. That's where he goes when he needs to think."

Emerson glanced around and then looked back at me. "Which way should I go?"

"Follow that path." I pointed in the right direction. "It ends at the garden."

He laid a hand on my shoulder. "Thank you."

I could tell how badly he was hurting, and I knew my brother was at least as bad off. "He needs you."

"I know." Most men would run from King. Emerson clearly belonged with him, like I belonged with Jax.

Emerson turned to look at Jax. "Are you going to follow me?"

Hell no. "He's going to stay right here with me. I sent another guard to keep an eye on King. I'll let him know you're on your way."

As soon as Emerson was gone, Jax turned to me. I could feel anger rolling off him. "Why didn't you stay hidden?"

"Because my stubborn brother needs him, and I wanted to encourage him because…"

He scowled at me. "Because why?"

Why did Emerson have to choose that moment to come out? If I'd been able to remind Jax of how powerful an orgasm I could give him, he wouldn't be protesting now. "Emerson leaving gives us more time together."

Jax started to speak, but I cut him off. "You can't deny what's between us."

"I'm not trying to."

"Then—"

"I'm working for your family. I can't—"

"Then don't. Let me."

He growled. "You told me I was in control."

"I want you to be, but—"

"You only want me to be when I listen to you."

I looked up at him through my lashes. "Are you saying I'm a bad boy?"

"Storm." His voice was low and gravelly, but he didn't sound angry. He sounded like he enjoyed my teasing. A lot.

"You could always punish me."

He snarled. "I'll punish you for real, and you won't like it."

"I'll like anything you do to me."

"Storm, please. I can't risk having to leave here, to leave you."

"But you're not with me."

"I'm protecting you. Keeping you safe matters more than anything."

"You can do both, fuck me and care for me."

A growl rumbled in his chest. I was pushing harder than I should, but I needed him too badly to stop.

"Your brothers made it clear I can't have any kind of relationship with someone I'm protecting."

"I can talk to them."

"No. I won't have you risk that."

"Then we'll keep it secret."

He sighed. "Are you this exhausting when you argue with them?"

"I'm worse."

Before he could respond, my phone buzzed. Considering everything that was currently going on with the family, I couldn't ignore it. When I pulled it from my pants and saw the name on the screen, I groaned.

"What is it?" Jax was all business again, ready to leap into action. I thought again about how he'd so casually asserted that he could defeat King. He really would do anything for me. My brothers would never have to worry about my safety if Jax and I were mated. If only I could make him see how strong our connection was. If only we really were fated mates, but that had just been a delusion, hadn't it? I'd just been lust-crazed and overly hopeful when we'd been together before.

"It's Trent, the bear shifter who manages Shifting Sophistication, our escort service. He's been trying to get me to go out with him for ages, and I finally agreed."

Jax's eyes shifted, and he fisted his hands at his sides. "You did what?"

Ooh. I liked this jealousy. "Something's going on there. Things don't add up right in the books, and Trent keeps pushing to make changes, ones my brothers and I will never approve. King and Garrett have been too busy to make it a priority, and they don't want me looking into it, but Trent has wanted me for ages, so I'm going to use that to my advantage."

Jax looked ready to explode. "No, you're not."

"So I'm only strong and capable when I'm in bed?"

He gave a low growl. "You know I don't think that, but if this guy—"

"You'll be there to see that nothing happens."

I could see him warring with his instinct to forbid it and his desire to let me have the freedom I wanted. "If he even thinks about touching you, I'll rip him apart."

I smiled. "I know, but we have to be careful. The only reason we haven't fired him is because we can't risk losing our alliance with the bears. Their leader, Bernice, is his aunt."

"I don't want you going out with anyone, but if this man is—"

"So you won't go out with me, but I can't go out with anyone else. Is that how this works?"

He growled. "You're mine."

"Then take me."

"Storm."

I could feel his need. He was so close to giving in. "Take me tonight, and then I won't ask for anything else until this current crisis with the lions is passed."

"Will you actually let me control things?"

"Tonight?"

"Always."

"In bed, yes. But not otherwise. I tried to let you be in charge, but... I can't do that. I can't fully submit like that."

He stroked my cheek with the backs of his fingers. "I don't need that. I don't want you to just agree to things because I tell you to. I love your willingness to go after what you want."

"Even if that's you?"

"Yes."

"Then take charge of me tonight."

"We should just wait. Anyone could find us out here. King and Emerson could come back anytime."

"If I know my brother, it will be a while before they do, and he may carry Emerson off to the main house. He's got it as bad for Emerson as you have it for me."

Jax lifted a brow. "Is that so?"

"Yes."

10

JAX

I must have lost my mind to be considering this. If someone caught us, I would lose everything—the chance to protect Storm, the chance to be near him. I hadn't denied myself for months just to fuck things up now. But Storm smelled so good, and my body vibrated with need for him.

I was close to losing control of my wolf. He wasn't going to let me send Storm away, and the thought of doing so sent pain through me. The longer I denied myself, the worse I felt. I was hardly sleeping, and Mara, the Howlers' amazing cook, had been offended by how little I'd been eating for the last few weeks.

My need for Storm wasn't normal. It wasn't just about him being gorgeous and eager and able to take whatever I wanted to give.

Mate, my wolf insisted. *Our mate.*

I hadn't wanted it to be true because of our situation. But if I were honest with myself, I'd known from the beginning my wolf was right. Why else would I have felt so compelled to stay close to Storm even when I couldn't be with him?

"Storm?"

"Yes?" He looked nervous. Did he think I'd changed my mind?

"I think… I think we might be…"

"Mates?"

"You feel it too?"

His smile made my heart skip a beat. "Yes. I have from the start."

"So have I."

"What should we—"

I laid a finger over his lips. Knowing he felt the same way was enough for now. We were short on time, and I'd promised him we'd do more than talk. "We'll talk about this later. I'm not going anywhere, okay?"

"Okay, but I—"

"Go back to the tree we were standing behind earlier. Take off your jacket, then put your hands on the trunk, stick your ass out, and don't move." He looked so good tonight. He was wearing my favorite of his suits, a navy pin-striped one that fit like a glove.

Fucking him outside like this was insane, but it was better than me shifting and dragging him off with my teeth in his neck, which was what my wolf wanted to do. But if we got caught…

No. We wouldn't. I'd make sure of it somehow. I'd faced much worse odds than this. Neither of us could stand to be apart any longer. Storm was my mate and he needed this, needed me to—

Mark him. Claim him.

Not yet, but maybe soon.

I followed him back into the woods. He moved more silently than a human would, but unlike me, who'd learned to move without making a sound, the crunch of leaves still echoed around him. We needed to stay quiet if we were going to keep from being caught. That meant I'd have to gag Storm. There was no way he could be quiet through what I had planned for him. I wanted to hear all his cries and whimpers, but I'd have to do without them tonight.

Storm positioned himself like I'd demanded, and I reached around and yanked at his tie. He sucked in his breath, but he didn't speak. "That's right. You'll have to stay still and quiet if you want what I have for you, but I'm going to help you with the quiet part." I freed his tie and ordered him to open his mouth.

"Oh fuck. Are you—?"

I cut off his words by stuffing the fabric in. "No one gets to hear you cry out but me." I leaned close and nuzzled his neck before biting his ear. The gag muffled his yelp, but I felt him jump. "If you need to stop me, take the gag out."

He nodded, but the look in his eyes told me he wasn't going to want to stop, no matter how rough I got.

"Do you have any lube?"

He shook his head.

"Then you'll have to make do with spit." He kept the gag in and made no protest, so I unfastened his pants, yanked them down, and knelt behind him. He groaned loud enough to be heard through the gag, and I smacked his ass. "If you can't obey, I'll stop."

He arched his back more deeply, sticking his ass out toward me. My cock grew even harder than it already was. I wouldn't really stop, no matter what he did. I couldn't. The scent of him was driving me mad.

I knelt behind him, gripped his ass cheeks, and pulled them apart so I could give his hole a lick. He tensed, but the sound he made was muffled by the gag. I teased his hole with my tongue until he was working his hips, making me have to dig my fingers into his skin to hold him still. I pushed my tongue inside him, and if it hadn't been for the silk in his mouth, his cry would have woken the whole forest. When he dropped one of his hands from the tree and reached for his cock, I slapped his ass hard enough to make him jump.

"Keep your hands on the tree unless I tell you otherwise." He looked over his shoulder at me, and the desperation in his eyes sent a thrill through me.

"I'm in control. You take what I give unless you think you can't."

He narrowed his eyes at me and turned back to face the tree.

I breathed deeply, needing to draw his scent deep into me. Then I went back to tormenting him with pleasure, working him open and pushing my tongue in as far as I could. By the time I pulled back, he was bucking against my hold, and his balls were high and tight. He was already so close to coming. If I'd given him just a little more, he wouldn't have been able to hold back.

I rose to my feet and skimmed my lips along his shoulder, up his neck, and over the outer edge of his ear. "You taste so good. I'm going to fuck you now. It's going to hurt going in, but you can take it."

He turned slightly, begging me not to stop with his eyes.

I ran a hand up and down his spine. "I won't stop. Not this time. I'm about to go out of my mind with need for you." He groaned and pushed back, rubbing his ass against me so my cock fit right in the crease. I squeezed his hips to hold him in place. "Stay still. I'm in charge here. And don't even think about coming until I tell you to."

He whimpered, and I smacked his ass right on top of the handprint I'd already put there. He dropped his head back, and I imagined the sounds he'd make if we were free to fully let go.

I spit on my hand and got my cock as wet as I could before I positioned myself at his entrance. "Open up and take me."

I pressed forward, working into him slowly.

He was struggling to breathe. It had to hurt, but he wasn't making a move to stop me. I was desperate to be all the way in, so I kept going, filling him, stretching him. Even without lube, he yielded to me until I was buried in him balls-deep.

"You love this, don't you? Obeying me even when it hurts."

He nodded and whimpered.

"You can take anything, can't you?"

He pushed back, trying to get even more. I pulled out and drove in again, much harder this time. He sucked in his breath and struggled against my hold.

"Shh. It's okay, baby. Just breathe. I've got you."

When he'd calmed. I started working him again, slowly at first and then faster.

He drove his hips back, clearly ready for more.

"You shouldn't have come out here to tease me. You shouldn't risk yourself like this, and you sure as hell should never have told another man you'd go out with him. You need to be punished."

He whined in agreement.

"I can't punish you like I want to now. But"—I punctuated the word with a rough thrust that made Storm whine around his gag—"when I get a chance to have you in private"—I pulled out and drove in again—"I'm going to give you the punishment you deserve."

He protested, and I just laughed as I began to fuck him harder and faster. I wanted to drag this out, but I couldn't. It was madness to be taking him a few yards from the guesthouse when Emerson—or worse, King—could discover us any time.

"I'm going to come inside you and put my scent all over you so everyone will know you belong to me." Storm's breathing was rapid and erratic, telling me he was close. "You want to come, don't you?"

He gave me a pleading look.

"All right. You've earned it." I dropped my hand to his cock and stroked him. In seconds, his body tensed, and he began to coat my hand with his spunk. I pulled out enough to prevent my knot from locking us together, and I nearly bit through my lip holding in a shout as I emptied myself inside him.

He squirmed, trying to take more of me, clearly wanting my knot. "We can't be stuck together out here, baby." He made a sound that would have been a sob if not for the gag. "I know you want it. You like to be stretched. Sometime, I'll give you my cock and a dildo inside you at the same time. You'd like that, wouldn't you?"

He nodded, and I wrapped him in my arms, turning him to face me as I pulled the gag from his mouth.

"That was incredible." His voice was rough and scratchy. "You know exactly what I need."

My wolf preened, more content than he'd been in months. "I do."

"Are we really mates?" His voice was soft, and he sounded so blissed out. We needed to talk about how we felt when we weren't coming down from the high of orgasm, but he deserved at least a short answer now.

"I think so."

"So you won't leave? You can't?"

"I will never leave you, but we have to be careful."

"I know how to sneak around my brothers."

I wasn't sure he was as good at that as he thought. "Promise me you won't say anything to them before we talk more."

"I won't. I know we need to keep it a secret."

"For a little while, but if we're fated to be together, we need to tell them that. They might be angry at first, but they can't send me away if I'm your mate."

"They might try."

I hated the fear I saw in his eyes. "I'll take care of it."

"I want you to claim me, make me fully yours."

Yes, my wolf cried. I wanted that badly, but… "Not yet. Not until we can be together."

"But if we're already bonded, then King can't deny—"

"Shit. King and Emerson are coming back."

Storm stilled, seeming to listen.

"Get out of here, go around behind the house. Anyone who sees you now would know you've just been fucked."

He grinned. "It was so good."

I kissed him gently, then smacked his ass. "Go. Now."

I made it back to the front porch just before King and Emerson emerged from the path through the woods.

11

STORM

The night of my date with Trent arrived. I was dreading it. The man made my skin crawl, but I needed information, and I had to admit to enjoying how jealous Jax was. I could feel the annoyance rolling off him as we stepped out of the car. He'd been seething for the entire ride to the restaurant because he couldn't openly try to convince me not to go through with this date with Denny in the car. It was obvious, at least to me, that Denny knew something was up, but I didn't think he was going to say anything to my brothers. He'd helped me break the rules before, and I imagined he'd do it again.

Jax growled as we walked toward the door of Luciano's. "If he makes one move on you—"

"We'll be in the middle of a five-star restaurant. What do you think will happen?"

"I have no idea, but I'm ready for it." He laid a hand on my shoulder. "I know you hoped to make me jealous with this, and I'm adding it to the growing list of things I intend to punish you for when I get you alone again."

I smirked at him. "I'm counting on it."

Jax opened the door, and I entered. I had to remember not to glance back at him. People weren't supposed to notice their bodyguards, and if I looked at him, I might not be able to look away again. But I didn't need to see him. I could feel his warm presence at my back, and I knew he wasn't going to let me out of his sight.

I'd suggested this particular restaurant because it was one of my favorites, and I'd wanted to at least enjoy the food while having to feign interest in an asshole like Trent. Now that I was here, my stomach was all knotted up. No matter how fun it was to tease Jax, I didn't want to be here. I didn't want to sit across from another man, especially one as repugnant as Trent, and pretend to be interested in him. I was going to have to force myself to eat, and I probably wouldn't enjoy a bite.

"Mr. Howler, it's lovely to see you." Angelica, the hostess, greeted me. I made myself smile. "Thank you. It's been too long since I've had the pleasure of dining here."

"It has. Your companion for the evening has already arrived. We went ahead and seated him. I hope that is all right."

"Of course. I wouldn't want to keep him standing around waiting." I'd rather rip him to shreds with my claws, but she didn't need to know that.

"Shall I take you to your table?"

"Yes, thank you."

I could feel Jax behind me. His heat seemed to caress me, even though we weren't actually touching. I no longer questioned the idea that we were mates. There was a bond growing between us. I'd thought I'd need Jax's mate bite to feel this kind of connection, but I could sense emotions from him in a way I hadn't been able to before the night by the guesthouse.

My wolf responded to Jax's anger and unease. *Mate.*
Listen to our mate.

I couldn't though. It was too late to back out, even if I'd
realized this was a stupid plan. I needed information, and my
family needed the bears as allies.

Angelica led me to a corner table near the back of the
restaurant. It was in a quiet spot where Trent and I could
easily talk. If I'd been dining with Jax, I would've welcomed
the atmosphere. As it was, I wished we'd been placed next to
a noisy crowd. Jax positioned himself against the wall oppo-
site our table as Trent openly looked me up and down. I had
to resist the urge to shudder. When he rose and held out his
hand, I heard a low growl from Jax.

This was a huge mistake. I prayed Jax could hold on to
his control.

Trent held my hand much longer than necessary, and I
had to practically yank it out of his grip. I could feel Jax's
fury through our mate bond. I worried he would rip out
Trent's throat if the man touched me again.

"Good evening," Trent said, giving me a knowing smile
as we seated ourselves. "I'm glad you finally agreed to this. I
knew you'd eventually give in."

Bringing this bastard down was going to feel so good. I
gave him a smile anyone with sense would see was fake. "I
had to wait for a chance to sneak away without my brothers
noticing. They're very overprotective."

"So your brothers don't know you're here?" His lasciv-
ious smile made me nauseous.

If he thought that meant he could force himself on me, he
was so wrong. "There's no need for them to know all my
business."

"Good, because I have plans for us after dinner."

My wolf snarled inside, and I wanted to gag at the

thought of his plans, but I smiled instead and twirled one of my curls around a finger. "That sounds… interesting."

Our server appeared. Trent ordered a gin and tonic, and I asked for sparkling water with lime and the calamari appetizer. I wasn't actually hungry, but having food on the table would give me something to focus on other than Trent.

"Don't you want a cocktail?" Trent asked.

"No, thank you." I rarely drank more than a glass or two of wine with a meal, and I wasn't about to risk being intoxicated around Trent. Jax would keep me safe no matter what, but I was sure Trent hoped I would spill some family secrets.

"Are you sure? There's no need for you to drive tonight."

Did he think I'd get in a car with him? "Of course not. I have my driver waiting outside, but I like to keep my head clear when I'm getting to know someone."

"I think we already know each other well enough."

From what I'd been able to tell during our limited contact, he thought I was an empty-headed pretty boy who depended on his brothers to do his thinking for him. I suddenly needed to see Jax, not just feel his anger. I dropped my napkin and bent to retrieve it. Jax raised his brows when I made eye contact with him, and I knew if I gave any signal that I was in distress, he'd be there in a second with a clawed hand wrapped around Trent's throat. Seeing him made me feel better. I shook my head, indicating I was fine, and Jax's face settled back into his impassive bodyguard expression.

Our server brought our drinks and calamari, and we placed our orders for entrees. After a few sips of his drink, Trent said, "We can get to know each other better, if that's what you'd like." Condescending bastard. "Tell me more about the things you do to help out your brothers with their businesses."

I fought the urge to snap at him. He wasn't even trying to

hide the fact that he thought of me as nothing more than a pretty accessory for the Howler family, but I had to remind myself not to let my anger cause me to reveal too much. "I handle all the communications with vendors for Tooth and Claw, Scandal"—a second club we owned that wasn't kink-focused and welcomed humans—"and the two restaurants we own. I also handle the scheduling and the hiring of front- and back-end managers."

"Sounds like they're keeping you busy." He was clearly humoring me.

"And what about you? How do you assist your family? I'm sure your duties at our escort service can't take up all your time."

He scowled but then covered it quickly. *Damn right I've noticed you aren't earning your keep.*

"I take care of scheduling guests and private parties for our casinos."

He continued on, bragging about celebrities he'd brought in and how successful his family was. They were well off, but nowhere near as rich or powerful as we were. At least I had the calamari to distract me. I just wished the company was better so I could truly enjoy it. I was absolutely coming back here soon with Jax as my date, as well as my bodyguard.

Trent's phone rang while he was in the middle of a story about how he'd saved the day at one of his aunt's private parties. He glanced at the screen and then back at me. "It's my brother. I have to take it."

I gave him the sweet smile he no doubt expected. "No problem. I know how pressing family business can be."

Except I'd seen the name on his screen. It wasn't his brother. It was Rutherford, a former client of our escort service, one we'd banned for not respecting our escorts' limits.

The business had been far from savory when my father was still alive, but since King had taken over, he'd made sure all our escorts were over eighteen and that they were working for us because they wanted to. We vetted our clients, and we'd instituted a zero-tolerance policy on any abusive behavior.

Trent was the only person who'd argued with the changes. He would have been happy to provide the underage escorts some clients asked for and to encourage—aka blackmail—men and women to work for us. We all wanted him gone, but we needed to keep him on to appease his aunt, so we simply refused to listen to his vile suggestions.

I couldn't catch much of the former client's side of the conversation, but Trent mentioned a party and plans being all set, and he told the man not to worry. "It's going to be exactly what you were looking for... Yes... Payment in full... Right." He ended the call after that. Whatever this was about, I had a feeling it was going to lead me to solving the issues with the bookkeeping and staffing at Shifting Sophistication. And if Trent had harmed anyone who worked for us, I'd let Jax loose on him, no matter what it meant for us politically.

"So how is your brother?" I asked.

Trent gave me another condescending smile. "He's fine. He was just having a little trouble at Lucky's."

That was their flashiest casino. The one where Bernice usually worked. I really hoped she wasn't involved in whatever was going on. We didn't want a war with the bears on our hands.

Our entrees came, then a few moments later Trent excused himself to use the bathroom, and the idiot left his phone right on the table. I waited until he'd disappeared down the hall where the restrooms were located, then I grabbed his phone.

Jax was by my side in less than a second. "What's going on?"

"Trent lied about who called him, and I'm hoping to find out more information."

His phone was locked. He wasn't that much of an idiot, but there were several notifications on his screen, including a few from the asshole client of ours.

You better deliver what you promised.

Half up front. That's all you get.

And then, finally something concrete. *Tonight. Lucky's. 11:00.*

I could easily guess that what Trent had promised to deliver were escorts, ones who would be expected to break the rules we had at our agency.

I turned to Jax. "Give me five minutes, then say there's an emergency and we have to leave."

Jax shook his head. "I want to take you home now."

"We can't just disappear."

He growled, but he went back to his spot against the wall.

It was all I could do to smile and listen to Trent's continued bragging. I was counting the seconds until Jax would help me escape.

Trent scowled when Jax approached the table.

"Excuse me," Jax said. His voice was even, but I could feel his anger and see it in his tense posture. "There's an emergency at home that requires Mr. Howler's presence."

"Are you sure?" Trent asked. "I bet his brothers can handle it."

Jax growled. "He's needed at home."

Trent's eyes shifted, and I stood quickly, wanting to head off a fight. "Jax is just protecting me. That's his job, and if my brothers need me, I have to go."

Trent still looked annoyed. "Then go, but I'm going to get you alone one of these days."

"Perhaps. Call me later."

Jax took my arm and tugged. I didn't think he could hold his wolf back much longer. "Good night," I called to Trent as I let Jax lead me away.

12

JAX

It was a good thing Storm didn't resist my attempts to remove him from the restaurant. I wouldn't have been able to last much longer with that disgusting man ogling my mate. I'd managed to remain impassive in front of far more threatening and horrific situations, but when it came to Storm, my control was shit. No one was allowed to look at my mate like he existed for their pleasure—not to mention how Trent had treated Storm like his head was full of fluff.

I laid a hand against Storm's back, urging him to walk faster. I'd messaged Denny to tell him to bring the car around, and he was waiting just outside the door. Normally, I rode up front with Denny while Storm, Emerson, or whoever else I was guarding rode in back. But I slid into the back seat beside Storm. I needed to be where I could touch him. If Denny told anyone, we'd deal with the consequences. Storm was my mate, and we weren't going to be able to hide that for long.

"Is everything okay?" Denny asked once the car door was shut.

"I was with Trent from the escort service," Storm replied.

"What?" Denny's mouth fell open.

"Just drive," I growled.

"He's up to something. The books haven't added up for months, and we've had several people quit. Now I think I may know what's going on. He's hosting private parties and using our escorts."

"Are you sure?" I asked.

"Not completely, but it fits with everything he said and what I saw on his phone."

"You checked out his phone?" Denny asked.

"I sure did."

"Good for you."

I snarled. "This isn't a game."

Storm laid a hand on my thigh. "I know it's not. Calm down."

"We need to tell your brothers."

"Not yet. There's enough pressure already with all the shit with the lions' leader pushing to take King's position. I can handle this."

I glared at him. "We'll talk about this more at home."

Denny smiled at me in the rearview mirror. "Don't mind me."

"Later," I growled.

Storm took my hand, and we passed the rest of the ride in silence.

When we reached home, we said good night to Denny, and Storm suggested we go for a walk. "No one will question me wanting some exercise or you insisting on accompanying me."

He was right, so we took one of the paths that led into the woods at the back of their property.

"I want to figure out what's going on with Trent on my own. Then King will have to acknowledge I'm capable of doing more than he lets me."

I understood why Storm wanted to handle this situation, and he was right that King had enough on his plate, but while Trent didn't seem particularly intelligent, he was still dangerous, and we didn't know who else was involved in his schemes. "Do you have a plan?"

"To be at Lucky's at eleven o'clock." He said it so matterof-factly. He was just going to show up, when Trent and probably plenty of other people would recognize him.

"Storm, that's—"

"The best way to find out if I'm right about what Trent's up to. There's no guarantee we'll be able to get any more information out of him, and if he's putting our escorts in danger, I want to know that now."

"No."

Storm glared at me. "You can't—"

"It's too dangerous. I'm not going to let you—" I knew I'd said the wrong thing as soon as the words were out of my mouth, but it was too late.

"You're going to behave just like my brothers, aren't you? I really thought you were different."

"Storm, I'm sorry, but—"

"What I'm suggesting is exactly what King, Bryce, or Garrett would do. Would you try to stop them?"

"Would you try to stop Shadow?"

"Shadow's… He still recovering from everything that happened to him. He doesn't even like to leave the property very often."

Storm treated Shadow exactly like the rest of his brothers treated Storm, but this wasn't the time to get into that argument. "Just because your brothers would take off without thinking this through doesn't mean it's the best thing to do. We need to do more investigating first."

"How are we going to do that? I can't ask Trent outright,

and you don't want me to see him again anyway. This is the only solid information we have."

"But we don't even know if—"

"Being there will let us know if I'm right."

I growled. "It's too dangerous. If they see you… If they think…"

"The casino is a public place."

"One your family usually avoids."

He tilted his head. "How did you know that?"

"I listen."

He huffed, and I reached for his hand. "I would advise your brothers not to go as well."

"Advise them, but not forbid them."

"You're my mate, Storm. You mean everything to me."

He let out a shuddery breath. "You have to trust me. You have to believe that I can do this."

"No one should go into something like this unprepared."

"I'm just going to a casino."

"To poke around and try to find out if there's a private sex party going on. If Trent or anyone else catches you—"

"You'll be there to save me."

How could he be so infuriating? "I'll be there, but I'm restricted by your family's need to keep Bernice happy."

"I could pretend I snuck out to see Trent."

"Absolutely not."

Storm scowled at me.

"There are other ways to figure out what's going on."

"None of them are as fast or easy as this."

"There is nothing easy about walking into an unknown situation with someone who's willing to pimp out teenagers. I've never been to Lucky's, so I've had no chance to case the area, find the best way in, or—"

"We just go in the main entrance."

"How fast will Bernice know you're there? Have you considered that she could be involved?"

"Our alliance might be uneasy, but she's not willing to anger King by messing in our business."

"Are you sure?"

He frowned. "Reasonably."

"That's not good enough for this kind of risk."

"I know where the private party rooms are. We could just watch the area and see who goes in."

"We'll just do some investigating first and find out more before we go anywhere near this."

Storm growled. "Of course I'd have a fated mate who'd treat me just like my family does." He started to walk off, but I grabbed his arm. "Storm, I know you're capable. I know you're strong. You can handle this, but not this way."

"King's a mess right now, between the lions and Emerson. Garrett's hardly ever here anymore. I can't figure out what's going on with him, but I don't want to add to his stress, and Bryce is picking up the slack for King because King's willing to delegate to him, even though I…"

"Even though you're the glue that holds them all together?

He turned to me, eyes wide. "You… You see that?"

"I see everything about you. You're my mate. For weeks, I've spent most of the day watching you. Do you think the guards don't hear or see what happens around them? Maybe some of them don't pick up on the nuances, but I do, especially when it comes to you."

I stepped closer and cupped his face in my hands, brushing my thumbs over his cheekbones. "I know how strong you are and how valuable you are to this family. I believe your brothers know it too, but they worry about you. I know that frustrates you, and I get why. You deserve the chance to do more without them holding you back, but that doesn't mean you have to run headfirst into danger."

He sighed, and I felt some of the tension drain from his body. I pulled him to me and hugged him tightly. We stayed like that for a few moments before he pulled back. "I should get back to the house before everyone starts to wonder where I am."

"Where did you tell them you were going tonight?"

"Out to dinner with a friend. They didn't question me too closely since you were going with me."

"And you aren't going to say anything about Trent?"

"Not for now."

I didn't like that. His brothers needed to at least know the situation was worse than they'd suspected, but I wouldn't push anymore tonight. "We'll see what we can learn about Trent in the morning, okay?"

He nodded, and we held hands until we got too close to the house to risk it.

13

STORM

I paced my room. The minutes seemed to creep by as I waited for the right time to leave. I wanted to arrive at Lucky's just after eleven so whatever Trent was planning would be underway, and I wouldn't risk running into him or Rutherford or anyone else I knew on their way in.

Jax was going to be furious when he found out I'd gone to Lucky's without him, but he hadn't seen the way Trent's eyes had lit up when he'd talked to Rutherford, and he'd never heard the demeaning way Trent talked about the escorts that worked for us or listened to him push to provide services that turned my stomach. I was all for anything consenting adults wanted to do together, but Trent didn't seem to care about consent or age. I wasn't going to let him hurt anyone who'd trusted that our agency would be a safe working environment for them. I thought of the escorts I'd interviewed who'd thanked me for caring about their comfort and also about Shadow, who'd been taken advantage of by someone who'd wanted to force him to submit to other men. He'd only been sixteen. I couldn't even think about what might have happened to him if we hadn't rescued him.

I couldn't wait when I knew Trent and Rutherford were out there forcing young men and women into Goddess knows what. Jax was right that it was too reckless to openly walk into Lucky's, but I was going to investigate from outside and do what I could to conceal my identity. I'd called a contact I had who'd worked at Lucky's, and she'd confirmed that, as I expected, the security inside was top notch, but Bernice wasn't overly concerned with what went on outside.

That didn't mean it wasn't dangerous for me to be there, but I needed to know what Trent was up to. I couldn't gamble on being able to get more information on his operation. If someone noticed me, I'd shift and run. I was fast and agile, and I'd stay alert to any trouble.

I wouldn't try to intervene on my own. If I had to, I'd call Jax. He'd come no matter how angry he was, and so would my brothers. If no one was in immediate danger, I'd confess to Jax the next morning. After he'd scolded me, he would forgive me and help me figure out how to stop Trent.

I didn't want to chance running into my brothers, so when it was finally late enough for me to leave, I climbed out my window and used a nearby tree to get safely to the ground. I hadn't left the house by this route since I was a teenager, but fortunately I was still just as flexible. I shivered as I waited to make sure no one had seen or heard me. It had gotten a lot colder since I'd come inside, but I was dressed warmly enough in a black hoodie and jeans. Once I felt confident I was alone outside, I pulled my hood over my hair and double-checked that I still had my sunglasses in my pocket as I made my way to my car.

When I reached the casino, I parked on the side of the building where my contact told me the private party rooms were located. It was twenty minutes after eleven. I waited in the car for several minutes. Not many people were around, since it was a weeknight and most people went in the front entrance. I didn't see anyone I recognized.

I put on my sunglasses and opened the car door. A gust of wind rushed in. The breeze was even colder here as it blew off the water. After one more deep breath, I stood and closed the door behind me. The security cameras would pick me up as I made my way toward the building, but unless they had a reason to be paying close attention to this area, my presence shouldn't draw attention. I didn't go inside. Instead, I moved around the outside, listening to see if I could detect whether any of the private rooms were being used. There could be events other than the one I suspected Trent was hosting, but all I could do was look and listen.

After I reached the side of the casino that faced the water, I heard more noise, music and the murmur of voices. It wasn't coming from the room closest to me though. The gathering was on the floor above.

I found some exterior stairs that led to a terrace and climbed them slowly, making sure no one was outside. I didn't think they would be on a night this windy, especially not in a place where you could still smoke indoors, but I didn't want to take chances.

The terrace was clear, so I moved closer to the windows. I wasn't surprised to see the curtains were drawn, considering what I expected they were up to, but I hoped at least one of them would be cracked enough for me to see in.

I approached the windows cautiously. After a few tries, I found one that allowed me to see a small section of the room. Many of the people inside were naked or nearly so, though fortunately, when I located Trent standing in a corner observing, he was fully dressed. The glare on the window made it difficult to see clearly, and the light in the room was low. I recognized another problem client, who was being sucked off by two women who looked very young, but I had no way to know if they were truly underage.

I saw an escort we'd hired recently who was noticeable because of his fire-red hair. He disappeared from view after talking with a man who looked angry with him. A few moments later, I heard a nearby door swing open. I tensed, but it was the red-headed young man, now wearing sweats and a t-shirt. He never even looked my way. He just raced down the stairs and ran. Shit. What had happened to him in there? I turned back, hoping to recognize someone else or see something that would give me a better idea of whether the escorts were there by choice.

"What the hell are you doing?"

I turned to see a huge bear shifter coming toward me. Fuck, where had he come from? I hadn't heard a thing. I'd been too focused on what was going on inside.

His fingers were already changing into long, wicked claws. He'd be on me before I could even shift into my wolf form, and he was between me and the stairs. I looked toward the railing. I could jump, but I'd be landing on pavement, and chances were I'd be too injured to run before the bear shifter caught me.

I stood there frozen, wondering if the bear would kill me or take me to Trent or what?

"Listen, I—"

The bear shifter's mouth dropped open, and he fell to the ground twitching as his hands became human again. When I looked up to see what had happened, Jax stood over him holding a gun.

I wanted to call to him and tell him not to kill the man, but any sound I made might alert the people inside. Jax fired the gun again, and a dart lodged in the man's neck. The bear shifter growled and tried to reach up for Jax, but Jax took a step back, evading him easily. A few seconds later, the man turned fully human and slumped back to the ground, seemingly unconscious.

Jax nudged him with his foot, but the man didn't respond. When Jax focused on me again, I wanted to run to him, but I was frozen in place, scared of what had almost happened and of what Jax thought of me now.

Jax held his finger to his lips to remind me to be quiet, and then he stretched out his hand. Having him reach for me gave me the courage to move. I walked quickly to him, and he led me back through the parking lot. When we reached my car, he motioned for me to get in the passenger side. I handed him the key, and he drove us a little way down the street before pulling into an empty parking lot and cutting the engine.

I tensed, waiting for him to yell at me, but he kept his voice low and steady, which was almost worse. "Why, Storm? Why did you come here without me?"

"Because…" *You wouldn't come with me.* "Was that natcylid you used on him?"

"Yes." Natcylid prevented shifters from taking their animal form, and it also caused nerve pain and knocked them out at high enough doses.

"Where did you get it?" I knew he wouldn't let me get away with distracting him for long.

"I have my sources, and I only use it in emergencies. Like when I have to rescue my mate after he does something incredibly stupid."

The tears I'd been fighting started to roll down my cheeks. Forget trying to explain or justify. I just wanted him to forgive me. "I'm so sorry. I was… I was wrong. I shouldn't have gone by myself. I didn't even… I saw Trent, but I can't prove…" My breath hitched, and I couldn't seem to fill my lungs anymore. Tears streamed down my face as Jax pulled me to him and held me tight against his chest.

"I'm so glad I was there. Seeing you in danger like that... It nearly killed me."

"You were amazing," I forced the words out between sobs. "How did you even know I was here?"

"After we said good night and you went upstairs, I waited near your car."

I frowned at him. "You knew I was going to do this, even after I said..." I trailed off as he raised his brows.

"I felt your agitation. I know we're not bonded yet, but—"

"I know. I can feel things from you too."

"And you're stubborn, Storm, as much as any of your brothers. You'd decided this was the right thing to do, so you did it. I should have made you promise me. That might have swayed you, because I know you take giving your word very seriously, but even then, I would have waited for you in case."

"Thank you. I know that's not enough to say, but —"

"It's enough for now." He kissed the top of my head and held me until I was all cried out. When I sat back, he brushed the tears from my eyes.

"Can you f-forgive me? I... I know I'm—"

"Yes, I forgive you. You're my mate, and you are strong and capable, but you were reckless tonight. You put yourself in danger and scared me and yourself. If I hadn't been here—"

"I would probably be dead."

Pain flashed in Jax's eyes. "That's... I can't even handle thinking about that."

"But you *were* here. You saved me."

"If you'd listened to me to start with..."

"I know. I want my brothers to treat me like I'm actually a responsible adult all the time, not just when it's convenient to them. I wanted to prove that I could take care of this on my own, but I guess I'm just a fucking reckless kid after all."

"No." Jax gripped my chin and forced me to look at him. "You made a bad decision. I'm sure your brothers would have done the same."

I considered the number of times my older brothers had walked into danger, sometimes with good reason, sometimes —especially when they were younger—just because they could.

"They have, but I knew you'd be angry, and I did it anyway, and now I need…"

"What do you need?" He tightened his grip on me as he held my gaze. His expression hardened, and I drew in a shaky breath.

"I need to be punished."

He gave a stiff nod. "You're right. You do. You need to be punished hard enough that you won't forget how wrong it was to risk yourself like this."

It would feel so good to surrender to him, to let him care for me in a way that would relieve the tension between us. "I was wrong. I hurt you, but not in a good way, not the way you hurt me."

"When I get you alone, I'm going to push you right to your limits because you need that, and I do too. I forgive you, but that doesn't mean things are settled between us."

They weren't, but a rough, harsh punishment would bring absolution and so fucking much pleasure. "Please. I need you to go hard on me. I want to submit to you, to let you be in control, but I also want to be independent. I feel so mixed up. Sometimes I think I'm not docile enough to be a sub, but I crave someone telling me what to do when—"

"Baby, I'm a control freak. I want everything to go the way I plan it, but life doesn't work like that. I don't need you to obey me all the time. I just need you not to take crazy risks and to let me help you."

Did he mean that? I hadn't thought I'd ever find a man who could except that push/pull of independence and surrender. "Right now, I need you to make me pay for what I did tonight and to help me figure out how to be strong without being an idiot."

"You already know how to do that. You were just too stubborn tonight to remember it. You've been pushing back against your brothers for too long, and then I told you no, and you—"

"Should have listened." I should always listen to this man. He knew exactly what I needed.

"Yes, you should have, and your ass is going to pay for that."

"I love you, Jax." The words tumbled out before I had a chance to stop them.

His eyes widened, and for a second, I thought I'd made a huge mistake. Then he smiled and cupped my face. "I love you too. You know that right?"

"Yes," I said softly as he brushed his lips across mine in a barely there kiss. It warmed me, but I needed so much more.

"Take me to Tooth and Claw. It's closed tonight, and we can use one of the rooms. You'll have access to anything you want to use on me."

He raised a brow. "Anything?"

"I trust you." And I did. Completely.

"You know you can stop me any time. Your safeword applies even when I'm punishing you."

Tears pricked my eyes again. "I don't deserve you."

"You deserve the world, Storm, and you also deserve a sore and aching ass."

I grinned. "Yes, I do."

Jax pulled out of our parking spot and headed toward the club. As I lay back against the seat and watched him, desire began to overtake the swirl of emotions inside me. It had been months since we'd been able to take our time with each other, and I thought we'd have to wait longer, but neither of us could. We needed this.

He glanced over at me. "You look happy."

"I am. I'm thinking about how much I want this."

"You may change your mind when I'm making you suffer."

"No, because you'll be caring for me. I thought I might lose you after what I did tonight."

"We're mates, Storm. There's nothing you could do to make me walk away from you."

"But if you didn't want me. If—"

"I want you. The mate bond brought us together, but I don't just want you because fate told me to, and you behaving like a stubborn idiot isn't going to change that."

I reached for his hand, and he laced our fingers together as he pulled into the parking lot of Tooth and Claw. "Will your brothers find out we were here?"

"The security camera will pick us up going in, but I doubt they'll look at the footage. We don't usually review it unless there's a reason. There are a few security guards here though."

"Already noted."

I hadn't even seen them. How did he do that? "They might mention that I was here, but I can say I'd left something or whatever. I can turn off the cameras near the VIP rooms. I'll take care of it. Just trust me."

"I do."

Those words made my breath catch. "You still do? After I fucked up tonight?"

"I might even trust you more, because I don't think you'll do something that crazy again."

"I won't run off without you again. I swear. Next time we'll go after Trent together with better planning."

As we got out of the car, I could feel Jax's need like I had the night he'd taken me in the woods. His wolf was right at the surface. What would happen if he let his animal instincts take over? I wanted to find out.

I squeezed his hand when he reached for the door handle. "I can take whatever you want to give me tonight. I feel how tightly coiled you are, how you need to let go."

"I can't do that. I could go too far."

"You can with me. I'm your mate, and you'd never truly hurt me."

14

JAX

Storm let us into the employees' entrance, and I followed him from there to the security office. While he turned off some of the cameras, I stayed in the hallway, listening carefully for sounds of anyone moving around inside. I knew there were guards on duty outside who should have seen anyone forcing their way in, but I needed to be sure we were alone and safe because once I got started with Storm's punishment, I wasn't going to be as aware of our surroundings as usual. When Storm finished up, I told him to go on upstairs while I did a walk-through.

"We've had security here all day. I'm sure it's—"

"I told you to go upstairs. I want you naked and kneeling when I get there. It's my job to keep you safe tonight, and I'm going to do it my way."

Storm looked down at the floor and took a shaky breath. "Yes, Sir."

"Better."

I knew I was being overprotective, but after what had happened earlier, I didn't feel like I could be too careful. I headed upstairs once I'd satisfied myself that the lower floor of the club was clear. I checked the public areas upstairs, then each of the offices, and the private rooms other than the one Storm had chosen.

Before I opened the door to the room where Storm waited for me, I took a slow, steadying breath and tried to let all the anger and hurt I'd felt earlier melt away. Storm had made a mistake, a serious one, but I forgave him. I wasn't punishing him because I was angry, but because it was what we both needed.

When I stepped into the room, all I could do was stand there and stare at him. He was naked like I'd told him to be, and he was on his knees in the middle of the room on the cold tile floor. His curls were askew like he'd run his hands through them before he'd settled. His hands were behind his back, one clasping the wrist of the other arm. He was a perfect picture of submission, but I could feel the energy vibrating in him. His wolf was ready to struggle with me, to challenge me. And I loved that. I didn't want someone docile.

"Look at me, Storm."

He looked up as I closed the door behind me and locked it. His eyes had darkened with lust, but there was concern there as well.

"You're exactly what I want. I'm punishing you for what you did, not for who you are. I will never punish you for that."

"Thank you." He smiled at me before looking down again.

"Wait there. I know it's hard for you to be patient, but that's what I expect of you now. I know what I want to do to you, but I need to see what's available in this room. I've been taking some lessons on how to use certain implements you might enjoy." Even when I'd been telling myself I couldn't be with him, I'd read up on more ways we could play together, and asked one of the Doms at Tooth and Claw to show me some techniques.

Storm's breath hitched, and I couldn't resist glancing over at him. He was watching me now. "If you need —"

"I didn't ask you to speak. Now that we're here in this room, I'm in charge. You don't move or even speak without my permission."

"Fuck, that's hot."

I growled. "Are you asking for even more punishment?"

"No, Sir." He looked down, but there was no real sign of contrition in him—not that I'd expected any.

I opened the cabinet and looked at the options for restraints and impact toys. I saw everything I'd need, but for the moment, I only picked up a set of cuffs before walking over to Storm and kneeling behind him.

"I know you could break out of these, but you won't, will you?" For shifters, restraints were mostly symbolic, since our strength and ability to change shape allowed us to get out of most bondage. There were cuffs we couldn't break. They were illegal, but I had some, and I hoped we'd try them out eventually.

"I'll be good for you. I promise," Storm said.

"If only I'd made you promise that earlier."

"But then we wouldn't be here. We'd both be lying in our beds, wishing we were together."

I growled. "Are you saying—"

"I'm just telling the truth."

"No more talking." I fitted the cuffs around his wrists and clipped them together. Later, I'd use them to attach his hands to the headboard, but for now he was perfect like this, on his knees, hands behind his back. "Someday, I want to use xekrum cuffs on you, so you have no way to escape. I want that level of control. I want to know you're utterly mine, to torment, to pleasure, to fuck."

"I am yours. Do you have—"

"Yes, but we're not using them today." He opened his mouth again, likely to protest. "No more questions." I loved how Storm could take the harshest spanking I'd ever delivered and ask for more, but asking him to stay silent was way too much for him.

I rose and walked around until I was standing in front of him. "Look at me." He did, eyes filled with need. "The first night we were together, you told me you liked to be used, made to exist just for pleasure."

Storm's eyes widened. He started to speak but stopped himself. "That was good, baby. I saw your restraint. Do you want that tonight?"

"Yes. Please."

"I need to take the edge off so I can concentrate on your punishment, so I'm going to use your mouth to get myself off." I undid my pants and pulled my cock out before taking hold of his chin. "Open up."

He did, and I wrapped a hand around my cock while sliding the other into his soft curls. "I expect you to stay still and let me fuck you."

He groaned as I pushed into him. At first, I restricted myself to shallow thrusts, barely moving into his throat. He swallowed around me, giving no sign of struggle, so I pushed deeper. It took him a moment to adjust, but soon he was taking me easily. "Still an eager little slut, aren't you?"

He moaned around my cock. "That's right. You're dying to choke on my cock."

He looked up at me, eyes pleading. I could tell he wanted more, so I thrust all the way in and gripped the back of his head, pressing his face against my pubic bone. He held himself so still, and I marveled at how obedient he could be when he chose to. When he started to sputter around me, I let him go. As he sucked in air, he looked up at me with watery eyes and a huge smile.

"You like being used like that, don't you?"

"Yes." He gasped, voice raspy.

"Then open up. I'm going to come down your throat, and you're going to swallow every drop."

"Yes, Sir, please."

"So eager. You need to come too, don't you?" He tried to answer, but I pushed my cock into him before he could. I wasn't gentle this time. I drove into his mouth, fucking him like he existed solely to get me off.

He took it beautifully. The only time he struggled was when he'd gone too long without air. He was so fucking good.

Mate. Claim, my wolf insisted. I assured him I would when the time was right. For now, we would punish and pleasure our mate. I took a deep breath, soaking in the scent of his desire. I could sense how much he needed this through our bond.

"I'm going to come now, Storm. Take it for me like a good boy. I know you can." He struggled to free his hands, but I didn't think he wanted to fight me. He wanted to touch, to anchor himself.

"Don't come," I reminded him just before I spilled down his throat.

He swallowed around me over and over, the tight heat of his throat seeming to make my orgasm go on forever. When I was completely drained, I let my cock slip from Storm's mouth. He was off balance without his hands to steady himself, and he swayed as he sucked in air. I gripped his shoulders, helping him stay upright.

"You gave me exactly what I needed, baby. I'm going to unhook your cuffs now, and I want you to get on the bed on your hands and knees, ass up, arms stretched toward the headboard."

"Yes, Sir." His voice was small and shaky, so I brushed a hand over his cheek. "Storm, look at me. Are you okay?"

He gave me a blissed-out smile. "Soooo okay."

"Then do as I said."

I helped him stand, and he walked to the bed on wobbly legs. As he positioned himself, I cleaned up and tucked my cock back into my pants. I liked the idea of him being naked while I was fully dressed. It would make him feel more like I was using him for my pleasure. It would also make me less likely to give in to temptation to fuck him or cover him in cum before I was done with his punishment.

I moved to the side of the bed where he could see me, undid my belt, and yanked it from my pants. Storm's eyes widened. "Are you—"

"No questions." He shivered as he laid his head back on the pillow he'd tucked under himself. He was so gorgeous like that, with his ass in the air, all vulnerable and open to me.

"Don't move." I returned to the cabinet and removed the length of chain I wanted to use. While I was there, I also picked up a crop and a short whip with a forked end like a snake's tongue. The whip would hurt. A lot. I'd practiced using it with the Dom who was giving me lessons. He'd insisted I needed to experience any implement I intended to use, so I'd allowed him to give me a few strokes with it. They'd burned like fire, and even with my fast healing ability, I'd had marks the next day. I wouldn't use the whip until Storm was deep in subspace and primed for the worst of his punishment.

The last things I chose from the cabinet were more cuffs

for his ankles, a cock ring, and a container of lube. I laid the things I'd collected on a bench conveniently placed next to the bed. Then I attached one end of the chain to a ring bolt in the headboard and the other to Storm's wrist cuffs, making sure it was short enough that he couldn't pull his arms under him.

"You're gorgeous like this, all laid out for me." He whimpered, but he didn't speak. I stroked my hand along his back. "I'm going to enjoy putting marks on your ass. You need to pay for what you've done so you'll remember not to put yourself in danger again. Are you ready?"

"Yes, Sir. I need to be punished."

I stretched my belt between my hands. "I'm going to use a few different toys on you tonight, but I wanted to start with something that's mine."

Storm licked his lips as he looked up at me. "Please, Sir. Use your belt on me. I need that."

I caressed his back again. "Yes, you do."

15

STORM

I exhaled and let my torso sink into the mattress as I arched my back deeply and waited for the first blow from Jax's belt. I tried not to tense as I imagined the way it would sting when it slapped against my ass.

"I'm going to push you, Storm. I don't want to go easy on you, and you don't want that either. You have your safeword, and I expect you to use it if you need to. I want to take you to your limits, but I don't want to go beyond them."

I glanced over my shoulder and saw concern in his eyes. I loved that even when he was getting ready to mark my ass with his belt, he wanted to be sure I was safe. "I'll stop you if I need to, but I want you to be harsh. I want to hurt. I need that."

He bent and kissed up the length of my spine, making me feel warm and cared for. I let out a contented sigh.

Smack!

I yelped, jerking away from the sting. "Fuck, that hurts."

"You're not going to be able to stay quiet through this, are you?"

He hit me again before I could answer. I shook my head

as I gasped for breath. "I can't. I need... I need to talk, to scream."

"Then give me that, your cries, your whimpers. Beg me to stop if you want to. Just know I won't stop until I'm ready, because I'm in control, not you."

He brought the belt down again, drawing another cry from me. He really wasn't holding back. My ass felt like it was on fire, and he'd hardly gotten started. But no matter how much it hurt, I could do this. I could endure it. I pushed my ass out, asking for more.

He cracked the belt against my ass again and again until I was begging him to stop. "I'm sorry. Please. I'm so sorry I was bad. It hurts so much. Please!"

He paused and stroked my back. "This is for your own good. You need to hurt, don't you?"

"Yes... I... yes."

That's right. He kept caressing me, his hands so gentle. "Take a minute to calm down, and tell me when you're ready for more."

I buried my face against the pillow as tears ran down my cheeks. Jax stroked my hair, my back, my sore ass, sending pain shooting through me, but rather than making it harder for me to settle myself, it made it easier. I needed that sharp focus. I needed to give in to it instead of fighting. Just like I needed to give in to Jax's protection, to realize he wasn't going to stop me from being independent or taking on responsibilities. He just wanted to keep me alive.

"I... I'm ready."

"You're perfect, Storm. Absolutely perfect for me."

He slapped the belt across my ass several more times before stopping again. It wasn't just my ass that hurt. Pain seemed to shoot up my spine and down my legs, making every part of me throb with it. I wiggled my hips, trying to get away from it, but that just made my cock ache more. No matter how bad the pain got, I never stopped wanting him. My balls were full and tight and my cock was leaking precum.

I didn't know if he was done or only taking a break. I was tempted to ask, but I pressed my lips together.

Jax leaned down and brushed his lips over my sore ass cheeks, making me suck in my breath.

"Turn over," he ordered. "It's time for something new."

It was going to hurt like hell when my ass rubbed against the sheets. I could do it though. I could do whatever he asked.

When I was on my back with my knees bent, my legs spread wide, and my ass burning worse than ever, Jax fit cuffs around my ankles and attached them to the bolts in the side rails of the bed. When he was done, he let his gaze slowly skim my body. "Mmm. I like having you all spread out for me."

I liked it too. I felt so exposed, his to use, his to punish. "I like—" I pressed my lips together, remembering too late that I wasn't supposed to speak.

But instead of scolding me, he smiled. "You've been so good. I'll allow you to talk this time."

"I feel like I truly belong to you like this."

"You do belong to me. You're my mate."

"You're mine too," I said, wanting him to know I claimed him as fully as he did me.

"I know, baby."

"Thank you for giving me this."

He brushed a kiss over my forehead. "I've got a lot more to give you." I shivered, wondering what he intended to do. He reached for something, and when he held it up, I saw that it was a riding crop. "You took my belt so well. I'm going to use this on you now because I don't just want to punish your ass. I want you to feel me everywhere."

Fuck. He really wasn't going to show me any mercy.

"Look at me." I'd been staring at the crop, but I tilted my head so I could see his dark eyes. "I want you to remember that this is about what you need, about sharing something that makes our bond stronger. It's not about me being angry with you."

"I know. I need this, all of it, whatever you have planned for me." I took a shaky breath and let myself sink into the mattress, letting the pain from my tender ass ground me.

Without warning, he brought the crop down on my cock. The blow wouldn't have been hard enough to really hurt me somewhere else, but it forced a loud cry from me, and I struggled against my bonds.

"Breathe. Don't fight it, just feel."

He cropped my cock again. I tried to do what he said. The sensation was confusing. It hurt, but it also felt so good. My cock was desperate to be touched, even if it was by stinging leather.

I waited for more, but Jax turned his attention to my nipples, cropping one, then the other. They burned as he caressed them with the tip of the crop. Pain and pleasure swirled through me. When he slapped my nipples, harder this time, I arched my back and keened. The movement made fresh pain bloom across my ass. There was no way I could move that wasn't painful.

Jax kept going, slapping one nipple, then the other, until I was begging him to stop. Next, he shifted his attention to my inner thighs before slapping my cock again, giving it a series of softer taps, then a harsh, stinging blow. By the time he returned to my nipples again, I was squirming and panting, muttering nonsense as I alternately begged for him to stop, then for him to let me come. I longed for some kind of relief, but as the stinging blows continued, at random now on different parts of my body, I figured out how to let the pain flow through me.

Tension left me, and I floated, connected to the real world only by sensation and my bond with Jax.

The blows stopped, and I waited, my body thrumming with pain and pleasure and a need for Jax that was deeper than anything I'd ever felt before.

"You've done so well," Jax said, fingers playing with my abused nipples. I arched into his touch and moaned. "You deserve a reward."

Having him there caring for me was reward enough, but he took my cock in his mouth. The pleasure that zinged through me took my breath. I would have come instantly if I hadn't been wearing a cock ring. I lifted my hips, unable to keep myself from thrusting into him. He let me move for a few seconds, taking me so deep his beard rasped against my skin. When he pressed my hips back against the mattress, my ass burned, but that only spiked my need. I didn't want to disappoint him by coming without permission. "Please. I... Please."

16

JAX

I knew Storm couldn't hold back much longer, so as much as I was loving the taste of him and his soft cries, I pulled off and looked down at him. His face and torso were flushed, and there were red marks around his nipples and along his inner thighs. "You're so fucking gorgeous."

He gave me a blissed-out smile. "Love you."

"I love you too, baby." I unhooked his ankles and removed the cuffs. "You've taken a lot, but we're still not done."

"We-we're not?"

"You said you wanted me to be harsh." When I picked up the short whip with the wicked snake tongue and let it trail along his leg, Storm made a strangled sound.

"Y-you're going to use that on me?"

"Just a few strokes."

He shivered. "That's really going to hurt."

"I am supposed to be punishing you."

"Yes, but I—"

"Turn over, Storm. I want your ass in the air, ready to take what I want to give."

He did as I said, and I ran a hand over his red buttocks, making him gasp. "Here are the rules. You must stay still while I whip you, and you absolutely cannot come."

Storm whimpered, pressing his face into the mattress, and I was sure there were tears dampening his cheeks. "Use your safeword if you need me to stop."

"I… I don't want to stop, but I'm afraid I can't take it, or that I'll like it too much, and I'll come."

"I believe in you." I laid a hand on his back. "Take a deep breath." I felt his body expand. "Good. Now let it out."

He exhaled, and tension slowly melted from him.

"That's right. Relax into it, just like you did with the crop. I'm going to give you five strokes with this whip. Once I'm done, I'm going to fill you with my cock because I need that. I need to be inside you, to mark you as mine."

"Please."

"Take another deep breath," I ordered. Storm inhaled, and I positioned myself perfectly to make the first stroke. "That's good. Now let it all out."

When he began to exhale, I cracked the whip across his ass. He cried out, struggling against the chain that held his arms. "Please. Goddess, please. I can't."

"You can." Before he had a chance to protest again, I let the whip snap against his other ass cheek.

He sobbed and worked his hips.

"You're doing so good, baby." The stripes across his ass were beautiful. "Three more strokes and you can have me."

"No, please. No."

I brought the whip down once more, and he screamed.

"You need to hurt. You asked for this."

He sobbed. "I know. Jax, just take care of me."

That's exactly what I was going to do. I cracked the whip once and then immediately again. He cried out so loudly I was worried the security guards would hear and come looking for us. His ass bore a gorgeous crisscross of stripes. The skin wasn't broken like it probably would've been if I'd whipped a human in the same way. He would heal quickly, and I would have him shift later to speed the process, but right now, I needed him, and he deserved to come after taking so much pain.

"You're not going to forget what happens when you disobey like you did tonight, are you?"

"No. Never. Please, I need you."

"I need you too. I'm going to fuck you now. You took your punishment so well. You deserve it."

My wolf was growling and snarling inside me, demanding that I thrust into Storm hard and deep. My wolf wanted to take him, claim him, bite him and make him mine. I was going to fill him up with my cum and then watch it run down his legs. He needed to be marked by me, inside and out.

I longed to let my wolf take partial control. The thought of how Storm would react to the feel of my claws made my cock jump. But I was afraid of losing all control to my animal side. I couldn't risk damaging my beautiful mate.

"Jax?" Storm's voice was shaky. "Don't leave me. Please."

I laid my hands against his back. "Baby, I would never leave you like this. I'm right here. I just... I'm trying to make sure I have enough control not to hurt you."

Storm turned so he could look at me. "You'd never hurt me. I'm your mate. I want you. I want your wolf, your bite."

I shook my head. "I can't, not when you're out of your mind from pain and pleasure. I want you fully aware when I give you the bite that will bond us forever."

"I just... I want you. All of you."

"I want that to. Later."

"Then at least let your wolf out. Let me see him in you."

"My wolf has been trained to be a killer. He's rough, and he's—"

"Not going to hurt me. I can feel him, Jax. I know."

Was he right? Could I trust myself?

"Give me all of you. Your wolf, your claws, your fangs."

Yes, my wolf growled. *Can't hurt our mate.*

I unhooked his cuffs so he would be free to move any way he wanted. Then I slicked up my cock, gripped his hips, and drove into him in one rough stroke. He cried out, but I didn't give him time to adjust. I started a punishing rhythm, driving against his sore ass. He whined and whimpered, but he also pushed back against me, meeting every stroke.

"That's it. Goddess, yes, Jax. Let go. Take me."

I snarled as I drove into him, gripping his shoulders so I could jerk him back against me until I was half sitting up, pulling him onto my lap. I let my claws extend. They scraped over his collarbone and along his shoulders.

"Yes, Jax! Give me all of you."

My fangs descended, and I was so tempted to bite him, to claim him, but I knew he couldn't fully consent, as lost to pleasure as he was, so I held back, only grazing his skin with my fangs as I kissed his neck.

Afraid I would go too far, I let him fall forward again, pushing him down onto the bed so I could fuck into him harder. I placed my hands over his and pinned him down, sinking my claws into the mattress. "Mine. You're mine. I control your pleasure, your pain, everything."

"Yes!" Storm bucked against me. "You're my mate. I love you."

"I love you too." I reached under him and unhooked his cock ring. "Let go for me. Show me how much you love being controlled, owned, filled."

Storm cried out, squirming beneath me and fighting my hold. My knot began to swell. I let go of his hands and sat back, taking hold of his shoulders again. I let my claws prick his skin as I drove as deep as I could, locking us together and spilling my seed inside him.

When I was thoroughly drained, my claws and fangs receded, and I managed to maneuver us so we could lie on our sides. "Are you all right, baby?"

"Yes! That was… You trusted me. You let me have your wolf."

"You were right. You're my mate, and I won't hurt you. It felt so fucking good to share every part of me with you."

Storm turned in my arms as much as he could. "I don't want to put off bonding with you any longer. I need you to be fully mine."

"I know, but I don't want to claim you in secret, and I don't think you want that either. As much as they drive you crazy, you're going to want your brothers to know we're mates."

"I do, and I also need that full connection with you. I can already feel how happy you are. You're more content than you've been since we met."

"I am, baby. We both needed this so badly."

"We did. I'm sorry for going to the casino alone. It was foolish. I put myself in danger. I scared you, but this… you being willing to go that hard on me. I don't regret this at all."

"You don't have to risk your life to get this. You can ask for it."

He gave me a soft smile "Next time, I will. I promise."

I brushed his hair back from his face. My knot had gone down enough to let me pull out of him, and he turned to face me when I did. "You should shift to help heal your ass."

"I want you to shift too then. Our wolves deserve a chance to meet."

He was right, so we both shifted. His wolf was a mix of brown, gray, and white, smaller than mine but plenty sturdy, just like Storm. My wolf was huge and black, intimidating to most, but not to my mate. When we curled up together on the bed and dozed, I couldn't remember a time I'd ever been happier.

17

STORM

Even with Jax insisting I take my wolf form to speed up healing, I was stiff the day after he'd so thoroughly punished me for risking my life. Every time I had to sit down, I was reminded of exactly what he'd done to me and comforted by the warmth and strength of our mate bond.

As soon as I finished going over the weekend schedule for Tooth and Claw that morning, I searched through the employee files from Shifting Sophistication to find the young man I'd seen at Lucky's. I couldn't remember his name, but his appearance was distinctive, not only because of his hair, but he'd been wearing expertly applied makeup and a lace shirt. He was also the only fox shifter we'd hired. I found him quickly enough. His name was Corbin, and he lived in an apartment not far from the docks.

Jax was guarding Emerson that day, but I'd promised him I wouldn't go anywhere alone. That meant I either needed to ask another guard to accompany me or bring Bryce in on my investigation. Either way, I risked King finding out what I was up to. For just a second, I considered going to Corbin's apartment on my own. It wasn't the same as what I'd done last night, but I'd promised Jax, and I couldn't be completely sure Trent wasn't having Corbin watched.

Bryce had assured me I could trust him, so, I decided he was my best bet. I found him in the dining room. He'd been working at Scandal the night before, and from the looks of it, he'd stayed until closing and possibly later.

"Rough night?"

He looked me up and down. "I could say the same for you. You look worn out."

I shrugged and immediately regretted it as my shirt rubbed against the small wounds Jax's claws had made on my shoulders. They were mostly healed, but the skin was still tender. "I didn't sleep well. That's all."

"Uh huh. Should I ask Jax where he took you last night?"

Ignoring his teasing seemed best. "Do you have plans right now? Because I could use your help."

"My plans involve drinking coffee and eating until I'm awake enough to move."

"I need you to get moving sooner rather than later. We've got a worse problem with Trent than we thought."

Bryce set his mug down and straightened in his seat. "What do you mean?"

"I've been doing some investigating."

"Does King know?"

I huffed as I joined Bryce at the table. "Of course King doesn't know. If he did, he would've taken over himself or possibly delegated the problem to you or Garrett."

"If he could find Garrett. He's hardly been around for the last few weeks."

I frowned. "Are you worried about him?"

"I wasn't, but Shadow is uneasy about him, and you know he's the one Garrett talks to most. He won't give me any details though."

"Sounds like we need to investigate that too. But first we have to fix the situation with Trent. King has enough on his mind with the lions. We can take care of this."

Bryce studied me for a moment. "You did something, didn't you? Something I'm not going to like?"

"I went on a date with Trent."

Bryce slammed his hand down on the table. Claws shot from his fingers and dug into the wood. "You what?"

"He's gotten more defiant about the changes we've made at the escort service, and we know something's not right with the accounting. I realize it isn't as high a priority as King holding control of the Council, but someone needed to figure out what was going on, and this was the easiest way."

Bryce's expression softened and his lips curled up. "It had the advantage of making Jax jealous too, right? Please tell me you took him with you."

"Yes, I took Jax. I wasn't going anywhere with Trent without protection." Bryce didn't need to know what I'd done after the date.

"So what did you find out?"

I was thankful Bryce wasn't going to berate me anymore the way King would have. "I don't know a lot of details, but Trent is hosting private parties with our escorts, involving some of the clients we've banned."

Bryce's eyes widened. "Did he tell you that?"

"No, he took a phone call during dinner. He didn't even bother to walk away from the table since he thinks I'm just a pretty boy who doesn't have a head for business."

Bryce scoffed. "Sometimes I think you're the most informed one of us."

"Tell King that."

"King trusts you more than you realize. He just wants to keep you safe."

I rolled my eyes. "He's an asshole a lot of the time, but I know he cares about me."

"We all do. And so does Jax. When are you going to do something about the situation with him?"

I sighed. "I think were fated mates, Bryce. At first, before we realized that, Jax didn't want to risk being with me because it could get him fired, and then he couldn't protect me."

"And now?"

"Now, he thinks King will have to accept our relationship because mates can't be separated."

"He's right," Bryce insisted. "King would never try to keep you from your mate, especially now that he understands how that would feel."

"I just… I want us to be fully bonded before we tell him because then he really won't have a choice."

Bryce took a sip of coffee before responding. "And Jax doesn't agree?"

"No, he hates sneaking around, and he thinks we should tell everyone first. I just can't… not now. I want to at least wait until this thing with the lions gets settled."

Bryce moved around the table and laid his hands on my shoulders. "I won't say anything, but you can't keep this a secret for too long."

"I know. I just… I need to know King won't take his anger out on Jax."

"Jax has done an amazing job so far. King might grumble or complain. Garrett will probably say something inappropriate, but they like Jax, and if King can trust him with Emerson, he can trust him with you."

Before I could respond, Shadow padded into the dining room in wolf form. I wondered how much of our conversation he'd heard. He gave me a pointed look and nuzzled my leg, and I slid my hands into his soft fur. I glanced at Bryce.

"Does Shadow know too? About Jax?"

I knew my youngest brother wouldn't say anything to King or Garrett.

Shadow made a rumbly sound that I understood as an affirmation.

"He sees a lot more than we realize," Bryce said

"You're okay with it?" I asked as I scratched his ears.

Shadow's snout rose up and down. I expected him to settle against me, but instead, he transformed. "You and Jax belong together. That's obvious. Also, I want to help you take Trent down."

Bryce growled. "I don't want you anywhere near that man."

Shadow rolled his eyes. "You sound just like King."

I gave Bryce a look that told him to let me handle this before turning back to Shadow. "Are you sure? If I'm right about the worst of it, things are going to get ugly. Maybe you could —"

"Do you even realize you treat me just like they treat you?" He gestured toward Bryce as though he represented all of our older brothers. "You're overprotective of me, and you don't want me to take part in anything. You'd prefer to just keep me locked up here."

His words hit me like punches to the gut. Was I really as overprotective of Shadow as my older brothers were of me? "I thought you preferred to stay here most of the time."

"I did at first, but now that I'm ready to do more, no one wants to let me. No one trusts me to know what's right for myself."

That was exactly what I'd expressed to Jax. Did this mean I needed to be more understanding about how King treated me? I didn't like that at all. I might not be able to sympathize with King's highhandedness, but I was going to try to see Shadow differently. He could be as strong and capable as I was, even if he'd had a lot more trauma in his past. "I'm sorry. I guess I do feel protective toward you like they do toward me." I glanced at Bryce.

"Hey," Bryce protested. "I'm the most accommodating of all of us."

Shadow and I both laughed, but I noticed Shadow was shivering.

"Are you okay?" I asked.

He huffed. "I'm cold. That's all. You all worry over the littlest thing with me."

Fuck. Was I really as much of an overprotective prick as my older brothers?

"I'll grab you some clothes," Bryce said.

Shadow shrugged. "Just a blanket would be fine.

"Let's all go to the living room," I suggested. "We can snuggle on the couch while we make plans."

With all the uncertainty in my life—my relationship with Jax, the lions scheming against us, and now whatever was going on with Trent—I needed the comforting touch of family. It was something all shifters craved, but it was harder to get now that we no longer lived as packs. I was thankful to have my family close, and I hoped they could accept Jax as one of us.

We settled on the couch, and Bryce pulled a blanket over us. I hadn't planned to reveal what had happened the night before, but our closeness made me feel safe, and the words spilled out. I told them about sneaking out of the house and going to the casino, about what I'd seen, including Corbin making a run for it. And finally, I confessed to nearly being attacked by a bear shifter.

Bryce growled. "You should never—"

"Trust me. Jax has said everything you're thinking. I won't do anything like that again."

"He's good for you," Shadow said.

I squeezed his hand. "I know."

"I'm just glad he understands how impulsive you can be," Bryce snarled.

"What's your plan now?" Shadow asked, ignoring Bryce's anger.

"I went through the employee records this morning and found Corbin's contact information. I tried calling him, but he didn't answer. Jax is on duty with Emerson, so I was going to see if Bryce would be willing to help me track Corbin down."

"Great. I'm in," Shadow said.

Bryce growled. "I don't think —"

"Shadow being there might help Corbin feel more comfortable."

Bryce took a long slow breath. "When King finds out about this, he's going to lose his mind."

"I asked you to come with me specifically so when King found out he wouldn't give me a safety lecture," I explained.

Shadow huffed. "Bryce, you can just stay here if you're scared of King. We're perfectly capable of taking care of ourselves."

"I learned last night that's not always the case," I hated to say it, but it was true. "If Jax hadn't been there as my backup, I might not be here talking to you now."

Bryce growled.

"Fine." Shadow said, glaring at Bryce. "You better not tell King or Garrett though."

Bryce gave a dry laugh. "Trust me, I'm not going to say a damn thing, because I don't want them exploding at me, but eventually, we'll have to tell them what's going on."

"Once we've talked to Corbin, we'll hopefully have enough information to make a plan to expose Trent," I said. "That's when we'll talk to King."

Shadow stood from the couch and stretched. "Give us twenty minutes to shower and change, and we'll go."

"I really wanted more breakfast and coffee," Bryce groaned.

Shadow rolled his eyes. "Then eat fast."

LESS THAN AN HOUR LATER, WE ARRIVED AT CORBIN'S apartment. I tried calling him again, but his phone went straight to voicemail like it had before. Showing up at his home unannounced would likely alarm him, but I hoped I could convince him we wanted to protect him, not push him into something as bad or worse than Trent had.

We climbed the rusty metal staircase that brought us to the second floor of his building. I felt lucky to have made it to the top without the thing collapsing. Seeing how rundown the building was made me wonder if we needed to reevaluate what we charged for our services and the percent of commission we took. Bryce stayed near the top of the stairs while Shadow and I proceeded on. When we found Corbin's door, Shadow pressed his ear to it.

"I hear someone moving around," he whispered.

"Good. Let's see if it's Corbin." I didn't know if he had a roommate or not, but I hoped we'd get lucky and catch him at home.

I knocked, and a few seconds later, the door opened as much as the security chain would allow. Corbin's face emerged in the crack. Once again, he was wearing beautifully applied makeup. "Mr. Howler?"

"Yes, but you can call me Storm."

"What are you doing here?"

"I want to talk to you about the parties Trent has been organizing."

His eyes went wide, and he ran a hand through his ginger curls. "I... I don't really know anything about what Trent does."

"You're not in any trouble, but I saw you last night when you raced out of a private room at Lucky's. You looked upset. I'm hoping you'll be willing to explain what was going on."

"I... I don't think... He said that if we talked about it, we—"

"I intend to put a stop to what Trent is doing, but I need more information. If you talk to me and my brothers, you could help everyone who's involved. I promise you will be protected."

Corbin frowned. "You're not alone out there." I assumed he could smell Shadow and possibly also Bryce.

"You're right. I've got my younger brother, Shadow, and my older brother Bryce. We're all here to help." Bryce move toward us, an odd expression on his face.

"I won't let anything happen to you. I swear it," he said, his tone far more serious than usual.

Corbin sucked in his breath when he looked toward Bryce, but he didn't seem intimidated. He seemed intrigued.

"May we come in?" I asked.

"I... That is, I... It's a mess in here, but I guess so." He shut the door. I heard the chain slide, and then he opened it again.

Bryce stumbled into me as we started walking into the apartment. I glanced back at him and mouthed, "What's wrong?"

He just shook his head as he stared at Corbin. I couldn't

really blame him. The young man was beautiful, and he was only wearing a silky purple dressing gown with a lace trim.

Corbin led us through a small living room. There was a basket of unfolded laundry on the sofa, dishes on the coffee table, and teetering piles of books, but it was clean except for the clutter.

When we entered the kitchen, Corbin gestured toward the table, which looked like it was on its last legs. "This is the only place where there's room for all of us to sit. I'm sorry it's not much. I'm in school, and my sister begged me for money again. I knew she'd never pay it back, but I gave it to her anyway, and… you don't want to hear about all that. Would any of you like some coffee? I just made a pot."

"Yes, please," I said. Shadow declined, and Corbin turned to Bryce, but my older brother just stared at Corbin like he wanted to devour him. I kicked him under the table.

"Oh… Coffee. Yes. Thank you." Did he really have to be so obvious? We weren't here to flirt.

"We're interested in anything you can tell us about what happened at the casino last night," I said as Corbin pulled some mugs from a cabinet and poured our coffee.

"Trent's been hosting these parties for several months. I think some of the men who attend them asked him to set something up for them, but I'm not sure. He invites some of us who work for Shifting Sophistication to entertain at the party, but it's not like working for you. We're expected to do anything the men ask of us." He set our mugs on the table along with a cream pitcher and a sugar bowl.

"Trent also brought in some other escorts, right?" I asked.

"He did, and they're… Well, I'm not sure how old they actually are, but some of them barely looked fifteen, and some of them are human."

I bit back a growl. Bryce and Shadow tensed beside me. "When is the next party?"

Corbin frowned. "I don't know. He doesn't tell us more than a day ahead of time."

"What made you leave last night?"

Corbin looked down at his mug and tapped his fingers against it.

Shadow reached out and touched his hand tentatively. "We only want to know so we fully understand what Trent is up to."

He met Shadow's gaze. "I know. It's just... I agreed to these parties to make extra money. I knew they wouldn't be regulated the way my appointments are when I'm working for you. I thought I could handle that, but last night, these men were taking turns with me, and it just... got to be too much. I pretended to pass out, and they told me to go get some water and then get my ass back to them, but I couldn't do it. I ran before Trent made me take something."

My wolf snarled inside. "What kind of something?"

"He encourages us to take stimulants so we'll be peppier and able to last longer."

Bryce growled. "This ends now."

I laid a hand on my brother's leg. "We will put a stop to this, but if we go charging after Trent and making accusations, he'll deny everything. Then he'll go to Bernice and fuck up our relationship with the bear shifters."

Corbin looked so fucking resigned. Shit. He didn't know me and how much I cared for the people who worked for my family. I probably sounded calculating and unconcerned to him.

Shadow slid out of his chair and knelt beside Corbin. "When I was sixteen, I got taken in by an asshole who hurt me. Storm, Bryce, and their siblings saved me. They're good people, and they're trying to change shifter society for the better, but it isn't easy, and their alliances are important. They often have to work around some obstacles, but if they say they'll put a stop to Trent's parties, I believe them. You could help us if you wanted to."

I stared at Shadow in amazement. I knew he was stronger and healthier than he had been a year ago. I knew he loved his new family, and that he understood King's vision. But hearing him explain the situation to Corbin sent warmth all the way to my toes. I rubbed Shadow's back as I looked at Corbin. "I'm sorry if I sounded like I didn't care. I want to protect you and everyone else that works for us. Are all the escorts at these parties willingly, or is Trent coercing people into it?"

"He's not forcing us, at least not those of us who work for you. He's luring us with the promise of more money, but so far, he hasn't given us our cut from a single party. I've asked him about the money several times, but he keeps putting me off. I think he plans to keep it all for himself."

Bryce growled. When I looked over at him, his eyes had gone wolfish.

I clasped his shoulder. "We will stop Trent, but we need to find out who else is involved. We can't help the humans and teenagers he's bringing into this if we don't know all the facts."

Bryce snarled. "I don't want to wait."

He was usually more easygoing than Garrett or King. I wasn't sure if he was thinking of what happened to Shadow or if the way he'd been watching Corbin was responsible for his fierce reaction.

"I want to help," Corbin said. "Hopefully, Trent will ask me again even though I snuck out last night. I'm twenty, but I can look younger, and Trent says these men love that."

Destroy, my wolf demanded. I wanted Trent to pay as much as Bryce did, but Jax had been right the night before, and his advice was still right now. We couldn't make an impulsive move. We needed all the information we could gather, and we needed a solid plan.

"Corbin, if you'll let us know when the next party is and agree to go, I'll come up with the best plan to expose Trent and make him lose his status with the bear shifters. If he's keeping all the money, he's probably cheating someone above him just like he's cheating you. If he's running this scheme at his aunt's casino without her knowledge, she won't hesitate to punish him severely."

"Will I have to go to the party?"

"I won't force you, but it might be helpful. We'd make sure someone is on the inside to protect you."

"Not just someone. It will be me," Bryce said.

Corbin glanced at him, and I could tell he was utterly infatuated. The more interesting thing was that Bryce seemed equally smitten. That could cause trouble down the road, but for now, it meant Bryce would protect Corbin fiercely, and Corbin would trust him to do it.

"Bryce will be there," I assured him.

"Thank you," he said, but he was looking at Bryce, not me.

I finished the last of my coffee and set down my mug. "I appreciate you talking to us and being willing to help."

Corbin turned back to me. "I'll do anything to get Trent out of there. Shifting Sophistication would be a great place to work if it weren't for him."

Bryce growled. "I told King we needed to get rid of him ages ago."

I scowled at my brother, willing him to leave this discussion until later. We shouldn't say too much about family business here.

"I'm sorry you've had to deal with Trent," I told Corbin. "If it were as simple as firing him, it would already have been done. If he doesn't schedule another party soon, we'll figure out a different way to expose him." I pulled out my wallet, extracted a business card, and held it out to Corbin. "My personal number is on this card. If anything happens that makes you feel like you're in danger, call me, even if it's the middle of the night."

Corbin looked away for a moment and drew in a shuddery breath. "Thank you. I didn't expect… If I'd known all of you were so concerned, I would've said something earlier."

"You've told us now, and we're going to fix things." I rose then, and my brothers followed suit. "Thank you for the coffee. We'll let you get back to whatever you need to do today."

"I was studying. I've got a class in—" He glanced at the clock on the stove. "An hour and a half."

"What are you studying?" Shadow asked.

"I'm taking accounting classes at the community college. But I hope to transfer and get a four-year degree eventually."

"Accounting?" I asked. We needed a replacement for Trent, and Corbin seemed like an excellent candidate.

"Yeah. I guess that sounds really boring, but —"

"Not boring. Useful." Bryce said. "I suck at math, so I'm impressed."

I rolled my eyes. "He's not kidding."

Corbin laughed. "Math always came easy to me in school, but then… Well, I had to take a break."

"Good luck," Shadow said. "Thank you for trusting us."

"We will take Trent down for you," Bryce insisted.

Color rose in Corbin's cheeks as he smiled at my brother. "I know you will."

Corbin locked the door behind us, and we headed back down the sketchy staircase. Once we were in the car, I looked at Bryce, but before I had a chance to speak, Shadow said, "How long is it going to be before you call him? A few hours? A whole day?"

"What?" Bryce asked.

"Your interest was ridiculously obvious."

Bryce blushed, something I couldn't remember happening in a long time. "He's cute."

"Let's get this shit with Trent resolved before you start going out with him," I said.

He rolled his eyes "You're one to talk, fucking someone you're working with."

I growled at him, and Shadow laughed.

"Don't you dare say it's different," Shadow said.

How had he known that was exactly what I'd planned to say? But he was right. I'd already had to face being an over-protective ass with Shadow. I didn't need to also be a hypocrite with Bryce. So instead of protesting, I called Jax and filled him in on what we'd learned.

18

STORM

I kept myself busy over the next few days, working at the club, checking in on the restaurants we owned, and strategizing with my brothers about how to get more of the Council on our side. Every time I saw Jax, I wanted to pull him into my arms and beg him to give me the mate bite that would complete our bond. But I'd promised we could wait until I was ready to tell King. I wanted to keep my word, but now that I'd been with Jax again, my need for him was even greater.

A few days later, I was working at Tooth and Claw when one of the Crown brothers showed up saying he had a message for King. I told him I would be happy to relay that message, but he insisted he had to give it to King in person.

I told him that wasn't an option, and he lunged for me. One of the guards who'd been flanking him stepped in front of me to protect me, and the other got a hold on the lion shifter, but the asshole managed to free himself and take off toward King's office. Bryce had arrived to see what the disturbance was. He told me to stay there in case other lions showed, then went after the intruder himself. Jax came bursting in a few seconds later, having sensed that I was in trouble. I assured him I was okay, but he refused to leave my side until the lion had been restrained and brought to the security office.

Emerson was with King in his office when the lion burst in, and King almost killed the man in defense of his mate. Once we got the situation under control, Emerson left with Jax and Denny, and I sat down with my brothers to figure out our next move. But before we could make any plans, a look of horror came over King's face. "What's wrong?"

"I think it's Emerson. I think… there's something wrong. He's hurt. We have to go to him."

I grabbed my phone before he even finished his statement. Jax was with Emerson, and I was suddenly feeling as sick as King looked.

The phone rang and rang as my pulse pounded in my ears, and my lunch threatened to come back up. When Jax didn't answer, I tried Denny, but I couldn't get him either. They were in trouble. I could feel it. "His phone's going straight to voicemail. Denny's too."

King snarled and yanked himself free from Bryce's hold. "We have to go. Now."

"You haven't claimed Emerson yet, have you?" I asked.

King shook his head. He wanted to wait to fully mate with Emerson until things settled down with the lions, just like Jax wanted to wait to give me the bite I craved. Why hadn't Emerson and I forced the issue? If either King or I had been fully bonded with our mates, we would have been able to track them more easily, but even without that enhanced ability, we'd find them. We had to.

"I'm calling Arthur right now," I said. I needed to take action, or I was going to fall apart.

Bryce's phone rang a few seconds later. "I don't recognize the number, but I'm taking this."

I fought against the nausea churning my stomach as I listened to Bryce's side of the conversation. "Yes, that's my vehicle. What happened to the passengers?"

Oh fuck. There'd been an accident. Was Jax… No, he was alive. I was sure I'd know if he wasn't. I could still sense pain and uncertainty from him.

Bryce ended the call and explained that apparently some lion shifters had rammed their car into the one Jax, Denny, and Emerson were in. Jax and Denny were at the hospital in stable condition, but Emerson was missing, which meant the lions had him.

Mate. Find our mate, my wolf insisted.

I fought the urge to shift and run from the room, squeezing my hands into fists and biting back a yelp when my claws stabbed into my palms. I hadn't even realized they'd come out.

Go. Now, my wolf urged, but I couldn't listen to him, no matter how badly I needed to see Jax and verify for myself that he was all right. He was safe at the hospital, but Emerson was in danger. The lions wouldn't hesitate to hurt or kill him, and the longer he was with them, the less chance we had of saving him.

"I'm calling Arthur back and having him send someone to the hospital to check on them," Bryce said.

I almost insisted that I go; then I saw how pale King was. He needed me. "You're sure Jax and Denny will be all right?"

Bryce squeezed my hand. "If the human-run hospital thinks they will be, then I'm sure of it. They always discount how quickly we heal."

My wolf screamed at me to go anyway. *Mate. Need our mate.*

I did need him, but I would wait until I'd done all I could to find Emerson. That's what Jax would want me to do. If he was conscious, he was probably blaming himself for not being able to protect Emerson. If we found my brother's mate, then when I saw Jax, I could tell him Emerson was safe.

King wrapped an arm around me and pulled me to him. Even though I knew he was as scared as I was, his embrace comforted me. When Bryce ended his call, he hugged us both. "Just breathe. We can handle this like we've handled everything else."

We could. We'd find Emerson. Then I'd go to Jax as fast as I could. I didn't care if my brothers knew we were mates. I would tell Jax I was ready to confess everything so he could claim me fully.

The next few hours were harrowing as Emerson's friend Henley and Damien—the leader of the panther shifters who definitely had some kind of relationship going with Henley—assisted us in locating the Crown family's hidden den. I kept in contact with Arthur as we raced to rescue Emerson, and he continued to assure me Jax was fine.

When we reached the Crown's hiding place, we were shocked to discover that their leader, Leon, and most of his minions had already been taken out by Leon's younger brother, Aidan, and somehow, Garrett had known all about Aidan's plan. I had a lot of questions, but once I knew Emerson, King, and the rest of my family were safe, I took off for the hospital.

Arthur met me by the door and explained that visiting hours were technically over for anyone who wasn't directly related, but the doctor on call had agreed to give me a few minutes with Jax.

"We're mates. They can't make me leave."

"Unfortunately, they can," Arthur said. "Even if you were officially mated under shifter law, they wouldn't accept it. You have to be either a blood relative or married by human standards to be allowed to stay in a patient's room overnight."

Only then did it occur to me what I'd admitted to Arthur. He hadn't seemed the least bit shocked. "You knew? About me and Jax?"

"I did, but I won't speak of it until you're ready."

"Thank you. Do you think if I talked to them, maybe I could—"

"No. Shadow and I have done all we can. They aren't going to change their minds. You know how humans are. We're lucky they agreed to give you a few minutes with Jax."

When we reached Jax's room, Shadow was letting himself out. Even as recently as a few days ago, I would've been shocked to see my younger brother there. His presence still worried me because we couldn't be certain there weren't more lions who intended to move against us, but I'd seen Roc, the head of our security team at Tooth and Claw, in the waiting area. Hopefully he'd accompanied Shadow here.

"How is Jax?"

"We made sure he saw a doctor who actually understood shifter care," Shadow said. "Once he was conscious, they had him shift, and it did a lot to repair his leg."

"Is it broken?"

"No, but it was fractured in two places, and there's a large gash that needed stitches."

"At least he's…" The words stuck in my throat.

"He's fine, really, except for being groggy from the pain medicine. He might not be able to stay awake while you're in there, but he's been talking about how much he cares for you."

Those words made my eyes sting with tears.

"Go on in," Shadow said. "I'll be here when you come out."

"Stay with Roc." I was trying to do better about being overprotective, but I couldn't help but worry.

Shadow grinned. "I will, though I would be fine on my own. I didn't notice a guard following you in."

"You're right. I came on my own, but it's hard to break the habit of worrying about you."

"I'll hang with Roc. Come find us when they kick you out."

I squeezed his hand. "Thank you."

When I stepped into Jax's room, my stomach knotted. He was paler than I'd ever seen him, and he looked vulnerable hooked up to all the monitors. I sat down on the chair that was next to his bed. It felt warm. Shadow must've been using it too. I reached out and grabbed Jax's hand. "I'm here. I'm so sorry I couldn't be here earlier. I just... I'm so glad you're going to be all right."

All the emotion I'd held in check as I'd helped King find his mate poured out. Tears ran down my cheeks, dampening the sheets as I lay over Jax. A few moments later, I realized he was stroking my hair with his other hand. I swallowed down a sob and looked up. "You're awake?"

"Storm? Love you." The words were slurred, and his pupils were huge, but the fact that he was talking to me was enough. My mate was alive, and he was going to heal. I didn't care what anyone thought, I was going to tell the world that he was mine.

I sat back and brushed away my tears. "I was so scared. I felt your distress. But when the hospital called Bryce, they assured him you were all right. I'm so sorry I wasn't here."

"Shadow told me. You did what was right. King needed you, and I'm fine."

I did not think he was fine, but the pain meds might be making him feel like he was. He blinked and then opened his eyes wide as if he was trying to keep them that way. "'S so hard to stay awake."

"You don't have to stay awake for me."

"Want to." But his eyes were already closing again. I leaned down and kissed his hands. "They won't let me stay, but I'll be back in the morning, and we're going to keep someone stationed on your floor." I squeezed my eyes, fighting back more tears.

"'S okay. You should rest."

I was exhausted, but I doubted I'd sleep that night. I'd just think about Jax having to stay here by himself. I wasn't going to let him put off fulfilling our bond anymore. We'd get a human marriage certificate too, because I wasn't ever going to have someone force me away from him again.

There was a knock on the door, and a nurse stepped in. "I'm sorry, sir, but you're going to have to leave now."

My wolf snarled inside, and I almost growled at her, but it wasn't her fault. She was doing her job by making me follow the hospital's rules. I stood and brushed a kiss across Jax's forehead. "I love you. I'll be back tomorrow, hopefully to bring you home." He made a small contented sound, but I wasn't sure if he'd understood my words or not.

I walked down to the waiting room to find Shadow, and what I saw made me freeze in the doorway. He was sitting next to Roc, and he was laughing. I'd never seen him that relaxed with anyone outside the family. Roc was grinning and talking animatedly, moving his hands and shaking his body like he was demonstrating some kind of dance move. Shadow laughed so hard I thought he was going to fall out of his chair. I would've thought a man as big as Roc would intimidate him. Apparently, I needed to stop making assumptions.

Roc noticed me first. "Hi, Mr. Storm. I was just showing your brother this dance I saw on a video."

"It's hilarious," Shadow said, as if that hadn't been obvious.

"Are you ready to go home, sir?" Roc asked.

"Yes, they kicked me out."

Shadow stood and wrapped an arm around me. "I know you want to stay, but you won't be any use to Jax tomorrow if you don't get some sleep."

Roc took us to pick up some takeout since we hadn't eaten. By the time we were nearly home, I was ready to curl up in my bed, but my phone rang as Roc pulled into the driveaway. It was Bryce. King had fucked things up with Emerson, and I was going to have to help him get out of it.

I was ready to strangle King for being such a fool. Here I was, being kept away from my mate by stupid human laws, when my asshole brother had just sent his own mate away, saying Emerson was better off without him because being together was too dangerous for him. What bullshit!

So now, instead of heading to the hospital first thing, I was going to have to drive to the safe house where King had sent Emerson and see what I could do to make things right. If King didn't have any more respect than that for a mate bond, maybe I'd been right to start with, and he didn't need to know about Jax before our bond was fully sealed.

19

JAX

When Arthur picked me and Denny up at the hospital, he insisted on bringing us back to the Howler estate where he and the rest of the household staff could take care of us. I'd been shocked at first, assuming King would be angry that I'd failed to protect Emerson, but Arthur assured me it was King who'd extended the invitation. Normally, I would have protested that I wanted to be on my own, but staying at the Howlers' house would allow me to see more of Storm than I would if I recuperated in my own apartment. Not that I intended to lie around for much longer. I was already going stir-crazy.

I tried scrolling through action movies on Netflix, but I couldn't find anything I wanted to watch. Storm had texted me to say he had to handle something King fucked up, and when I'd arrived at their house, Bryce had explained that King had sent Emerson away. He'd wanted me to know that nothing less serious would've kept Storm from being the one to bring me home.

I needed Storm, but Bryce was right that Storm had the

best chance of comforting Emerson and getting King's head out of his ass.

That didn't stop me from constantly checking my phone to make sure I hadn't missed a message from him. I would have been restless stuck in bed all day in any case, but longing to see my mate made it worse. I barely remembered talking to him the night before, and I needed to touch him, to hold him, to see for myself that nothing had happened to him when he'd gone with his brothers to rescue Emerson.

I knew he wasn't ready to tell his family, and now that Emerson had been taken on my watch, I was no longer sure King would easily accept our mating. He might be willing to see me cared for, but would he ever really trust me again?

I wasn't sure how Storm and I would hide our relationship with all his bothers around, but we'd have to find a way. After what we'd been through, I didn't care how much my leg still hurt or how many stitches I had from various cuts—I needed to be inside my mate, to feel him come apart with pleasure.

Claim him, my wolf demanded. *Bite. Mark. Take.*

Suddenly, I caught Storm's scent. Was that my imagination or—

The door opened, and Storm slipped in.

"Jax." The relief in his voice sent flutters through my chest. I held out my arms.

"Come here, baby!"

Storm pushed the door shut and ran to me. I hugged him tightly, ignoring the protest of my sore muscles. His tears dampened my t-shirt as he pressed his face into my chest. "I could have lost you."

"You went after the lions with your brothers. I could have lost you too."

"I wasn't going to risk Emerson or let them get away with hurting you."

I took a deep breath, letting his scent calm me. "I love you so much."

"I love you too. I'm so glad you're mine."

"Yes. Need you." I couldn't keep the growl out of my voice.

Storm pulled back and looked at me, his expression serious. "I'm ready to tell my family. I don't want to hide anymore. If we'd been bonded, I would've known where you were when they took you to the hospital, and if King and Emerson had been, we would've found Emerson much more quickly. I can't risk needing that link again and not having it."

I squeezed my eyes shut. I wanted all of that too. "Are King and Emerson okay now?"

Storm frowned, obviously expecting a different response. "I think so."

"That's good. I... I know I said we should tell him and the rest of your brothers, but I failed to protect King's mate. Do you really think—"

"Emerson is fine."

"That doesn't change the fact that the lions took him when I was supposed to be keeping him safe."

"Jax, no one blames you, and King feels horrible about what happened to you and Denny."

"But does he want me to be his brother's mate?"

Storm growled. "It makes no difference what he wants. Fate has decided that you're my mate."

I felt a bond with him, I knew I did, but after waking up in the hospital unsure what had happened, not knowing where Storm was and then not being able to see him when I wasn't out of my mind with painkillers, I'd started to doubt everything. "Are we sure?"

Storm frowned at me, anger, fear, and determination mixed in his eyes. "Are you telling me you don't feel this?"

He gripped my hands. Heat shot through me, a comforting warmth as well as sexual heat. I didn't just feel him where he touched me. I felt him inside, like he was speaking to my wolf.

Fool. My wolf said. *He's ours.*

Why was I trying to deny that? "I'm sorry. I…"

"Did you hit your head in the crash? Because this doesn't sound like you. You don't doubt yourself."

"You're so wrong. I doubt myself every day, every mission, but I keep going anyway and never let it show."

Storm gave me a soft smile. "You always seem so together."

"I've trained myself to, but when it comes to you… I can't hold my mask in place."

Storm slid his fingers into my hair and massaged my head. I closed my eyes and let myself enjoy his soothing touch. "King is going to have to accept this eventually. You're mine, and nothing is changing that."

I knew that. We were fated mates. I wasn't really questioning that, especially considering how I felt right then with him in my arms, but I didn't want Storm to have to fight his family. "You wanted to wait before. Maybe you were right."

"No, I wasn't. I thought we should wait until things settled down with the lions, but now there's the shit with Trent and the escorts. Corbin could call any day, and once that's settled, there will be something else." When he pulled away from me and stood, I shivered, suddenly cold from the loss of him.

"Storm, I know things won't ever fully settle down, but I'm just not sure now is the right time."

"I can't wait any longer to be mated to you. My wolf

needs you. I need you, but you don't want to claim me until my brothers know."

Someone knocked on the door. Storm moved to the chair by the bed before calling, "Come in."

I braced myself. What if it was King, and he'd heard our argument? But when the door opened, it was Emerson. He looked from me to Storm. "I'm sorry. Am I interrupting something?"

"No, I was just checking on our patients," Storm said, his voice chilly. He rose from the bed, and I grabbed his arm.

"Stay. I think we have more to talk about." I needed him there. I needed to assess the risk he wanted us to take and make a plan, but he was right—we couldn't wait any longer to be fully bonded.

Emerson gave Storm a knowing smile, but I didn't let that bother me. If he told King, we'd deal with it. Anything was better than the anguish I felt through our mate bond.

Storm sank back into the chair by my bed, and thankfully, Emerson didn't question us further. Instead, he turned back to me and said, "I needed to see for myself that you were okay. Did you hear that I'm going to be a permanent resident here, so you'll get to follow me around some more?"

I forced myself to smile. "I'm just glad I'm still here to do the following."

"So am I. I'm so sorry that—"

He was sorry? "No, it's me who should be sorry. I should've known the Crowns would make a move."

Emerson frowned. "If King didn't know, why should you? I don't blame any of you. When they dragged me from the car, and you were lying there unconscious, I thought... I wasn't sure I'd ever see you again. I'm really glad you're all right."

"Me too," Storm said, reaching for my hand once again.

The tightness in my chest loosened. Things were going to be okay between us. I squeezed his hand and laced our fingers together as the three of us discussed King's stubbornness and how things had finally been smoothed over between him and Emerson.

"Is he waiting for you now?" I asked after we'd all had a laugh at King's expense.

"No, but he'll be here soon." Emerson got a goofy, smitten smile on his face. Did I look like that when I was thinking of Storm? If I did, it was a miracle everyone in the household hadn't figured out we were mates.

When Emerson left, I turned to Storm. "I'm sorry. I —"

"We can wait a little longer to tell King," he said before I finished. "I know he doesn't blame you, but he needs some time to finish getting his shit together with Emerson. As soon as you're healed enough, though, you're claiming me with your bite."

I frowned. There was something Storm wasn't saying. I'd learned to read him fairly well, and he was trying to gloss over details. "You said we can wait for King. What about the rest of your brothers?"

Color rose in Storm's cheeks. "Bryce and Shadow already know."

"You told them?"

"Not exactly."

I stared at him. He wasn't getting out of explaining this to me. "Shadow just knew, and there was no point in trying to deny it. Bryce could tell something was up with me. He's always been the brother I confided in, so I knew he'd keep our secret. I asked him if Garrett suspected too, but he doesn't know."

"And Emerson?"

Storm glanced toward the door where Emerson had just exited. "I'm guessing he probably knows now."

"Will he tell King?"

Storm shook his head. "He has better sense than that."

"What about the others? Will they let it slip?"

Storm shrugged. "It's possible. King will likely dismiss it if they do. He often assumes we don't know what we're talking about."

I took his hand and pulled him toward me until he was forced to sit on the bed. If King truly forgave me, then we would tell him soon. I didn't like that the others knew, but ultimately I was more relieved than disturbed by it. With Bryce and Shadow on our side, things would be all right. Storm, together with the two of them, could likely convince King of anything. Garrett was a wildcard, but if the others accepted me, he eventually would. And from everything I'd heard about what had happened with the Crowns, he had his own issues to deal with, so he wouldn't be able to invest a lot of time in arguing with Storm.

My mate wanted my bite, and I was going to give it to him.

Yes! my wolf cried. *Now.*

I cupped Storm's face and held his gaze. "You said you wanted me to claim you as soon as I was healed enough."

He nodded slowly. "I do."

"You're already mine. You have been since our first night together, but it's time for us to make it official."

His eyes widened. "You mean now?"

"I thought you didn't want to wait."

"But your leg… you're not healed all the way, and—"

"It's a lot better today. I've got a spot picked out for us, near where we were that night by the guesthouse." Shifters always preferred to bond with one another outside.

"That's too far for you to—"

"I have crutches, but I can walk on my leg if I need to. It's getting stiff from me lying here in bed anyway."

Storm narrowed his eyes. "When did the doctor say you should put weight on your leg?"

I waved off his question. "She said I should shift every day to help it heal, so we'll shift and let our wolves have time together after I claim you."

"Jax, I don't think—"

"I'm fine. We've waited long enough. We're doing this now." I let my wolf come out in my voice, and my commanding tone made Storm shudder.

"I should tell you no. You're supposed to be resting."

"Wrong. You should be an obedient mate and gather the things we need."

Storm huffed, but he didn't protest. "What do we need?"

"Get a blanket and lube. I'll take care of the rest."

"The rest? What are you planning? You really can't strain on your leg."

"Stop fussing and trust me." I gripped his wrist again, letting my claws emerge so he felt them prick his vulnerable skin. "From now until this is done, I'm in control, not you. Unless you say 'red,' I expect you to do exactly as I say."

Storm's tongue snuck out and wet his lips before he spoke. "You're really going to bite me now? Today?"

I let my eyes shift so my wolf looked out at him. "Yes. It's past time we did this. I'm going to take you to a secluded spot, and I'm going to make you one hundred percent mine. After today, you'll bear my mate mark always. You're sure that's what you want?"

"I've never wanted anything more."

"Then go get the things we need, and tell whoever needs to know that you'll be unreachable for the next few hours."

"Hours?"

"Haven't I always taken my time with you?"

"Yes," he squeaked.

"Get moving." He stood, and I looked him up and down. He was gorgeous in his dark gray suit, but it wouldn't do for what I had in mind. "Before you come back, change into something easier to get on and off."

20

STORM

When I rushed from Jax's room, I was so excited I didn't pay attention to where I was going and ran smack into Shadow. For once, he was in human form and fully dressed.

"Whoa," he said. "What's wrong?"

"Jax agreed to perform the mating ceremony with me."

Shadow's eyes widened. "Now?"

"Yes. I was going to find you or Bryce and let you know so you could make sure King doesn't come looking for us."

"Emerson's waiting for him in his room, so I'm fairly sure that is not going to happen."

"Garrett could come home. I don't want him asking questions either."

Shadow laid a hand on my shoulder. "I'll take care of everything. Just trust me."

This time, I didn't hesitate to leave him in charge. He was just as capable as me, and it was time we all started to acknowledge that. "I do. Thank you."

He pulled me into a tight hug. "Congratulations. You deserve this. And King will accept Jax, so quit worrying."

"How did you know we were worried about—"

The are-you-kidding-me look he gave me stopped my words. "You always worry too much about what King thinks. Now get going."

I raced down the hall to my room and quickly changed into athletic pants and a t-shirt. Garrett rolled his eyes every time he saw it, but I had a feeling Jax would get a kick out of it. I grabbed a tube of lube from my en suite bathroom and a blanket from the linen closet there and stuffed both into a tote bag before heading back to see Jax.

I got lucky and made it to Jax's room without running into anyone else. When I slipped inside, he was doing some standing stretches. "Are you sure you're up to this?"

The only answer I received was a growl.

"I'll take that as a yes." I paused and added a sassy, "Sir."

He raised his brows. "Are you asking to be whipped again?"

"Maaaybe."

He winced as he straightened.

"But it can wait until you're fully healed. You can keep track of my offenses and punish me really hard."

"You loved that the other night." He gave me a heated once-over, and my cock swelled, tenting my sweats.

"I did." He'd known exactly the right balance of pain and pleasure to give me.

He shifted his weight to his good leg and held out his hand. "Hand me the bag."

After he took it, he reached under the covers, pulled something out, and stuffed it in the bag so quickly I couldn't see what it was.

"I can carry that so you don't have to worry about it and your crutches."

He studied me for a moment. "No peeking."

"I'll be a good boy."

He huffed. "I'm not so sure of that."

"You like when I'm bad."

"I really fucking do." His grin sent sparks racing over me.

Jax grabbed only one of the crutches that were leaning against the wall by his bed. I wanted to question whether his doctor would approve of him not using both, but he was as stubborn as any of us Howlers, so he would just dismiss my concerns. I would make sure he rested after the mating ceremony was over, and even if he set his healing back a bit, he was healthy and strong, and I knew that he would be okay. Once our mate bond was fully established, I would be able to tell if he was downplaying the amount of pain he was in.

"When did you pick out a place for our mating ceremony?" I asked as we walked across the back lawn. I could tell Jax was frustrated by our slow pace, and I wanted to distract him.

"Right after that night you came to see me at the guesthouse and we both admitted that we thought we were fated for one another. I took a walk after I got off duty and found a small clearing. I knew it would be the perfect spot if—when I was ready to claim you."

"I love how prepared you always are."

He growled. "Then you need to show your appreciation better by waiting on me and trusting my plans."

I grinned at him. "I'm working on that."

When we reached the spot he'd chosen, I marveled at the way the sun filtered through the trees.

"Strip," Jax ordered before I could compliment his choice of location. His voice was low and rough as though his wolf was right at the surface.

I pouted at him. "I was hoping I'd get to watch you strip this time." He snarled, and it made me shiver.

"You really are wanting me to tally up offenses, aren't you?"

I grinned at him. "I am."

"Do as I said. Now."

I yanked my t-shirt over my head and tossed it on the ground. Then I pushed my pants down, letting Jax see that I'd gone commando. He stared at me, eyes darkening.

"Like what you see?"

"You know I do. Now help me spread out the blanket."

I took hold of two corners. We stretched the blanket between us and placed it on the ground. After bending to smooth the wrinkles, I looked up at him through my lashes. "What would you like me to do now, Sir?"

Lust burned in his eyes as he glared at me. "Are you always going to be this sassy?"

"Probably."

Instead of the growly response I expected, he grinned. "I'm counting on it. Now kneel, clasp your hands behind your back, and keep your eyes on me."

I dropped to my knees in one fluid movement, ignoring how uncomfortable the uneven ground was. As I watched, Jax lifted his t-shirt, revealing his broad, hair-dusted chest. I wanted to rise to my feet, tease his nipples with my tongue, and run my fingers over his firm pecs and abs, but I stayed right where I was. I could obey when I wanted to.

He pulled the shirt over his head, tossed it on top of my clothes, and then held my gaze as he pushed his pants and underwear down. I could tell that he was placing most of his weight on his good leg when he could, but he didn't falter once or even seem to notice his injury as he removed his shoes and pulled his pants and briefs off.

His eyes had shifted as he'd stripped, and I could feel his wolf pushing to take over. I wanted to feel the animal in Jax again like I had the other day. And I was thrilled that we'd have time to play and cuddle in wolf form once we were fully bonded. Jax wouldn't be up for a run, but we could do that another night.

My breath caught as Jax wrapped a hand around his shaft and pumped it up and down. Precum glistened at the slit, and I longed to lick it off. I drew in a deep breath, enjoying the strong scent of my mate's arousal. It wasn't enough. I needed to be able to taste him, his cum, his sweat, and the warmth of his delicious mouth.

I enjoyed the games we played, the pleasure and pain, the way Jax drew things out, but I didn't want to linger now. I wanted to feel his cock driving into me as his fangs sank into my neck, marking me as his. The need to be his mate seemed to be building until I thought it would swallow me whole. "Please don't make me wait, Sir."

"So impatient."

I groaned. "Can't you feel how much I need you?"

Jax kept working himself, smearing the precum over his cockhead with his thumb. "Are you going to listen to me and do what I tell you?"

He wanted obedience from me, so I would give it. "Yes, Sir. I promise to do as you ask."

"Good." He lowered himself to the blanket, and I resisted the urge to reach out and assist him. "Since you've made it very clear you don't want me to risk straining my leg, I'm going to let you do the work, but I'll tell you exactly what to do. You'll get to ride my cock, but only as fast or slow as I tell you. First though, I want to watch you stretch yourself, and I have something else for you to play with."

I fluttered my lashes at him. "Will you tell me what it is, please, Sir?"

"You wouldn't fool anyone with that innocent act."

I laughed. "It makes you smile though."

"It does. Grab the bag and look inside."

I did as he said. There was a sizable dildo inside. "You want to watch me fuck myself with it?"

"Yes. And then I'm going to fuck you with it and my cock."

I glanced between the dildo and Jax's thick shaft and lost the ability to breathe at the thought of how taking them both would make my ass ache. "Wow."

Jax grinned. "You love having your ass stretched, so I'm going to give you more of what you enjoy."

"Yes, please."

When he laid on his back and stretched, showing off his muscles for me, I grabbed the lube and the dildo and laid them beside him.

"Straddle my thighs facing away from me so I can watch as you open yourself with your fingers and then with the toy I brought you."

I positioned myself as he'd said, squirted lube on the fingers of one hand, and used the other to spread my ass and give him a better view. I sucked in my breath as I teased my rim and worked first one finger and then another inside me.

Jax groaned, and I began moving up and down, fucking myself on my fingers. From the sound of his labored breathing, I was giving him a good show.

"Use the dildo now. I want to see your hole stretched around it."

That was a command I could obey easily. I slicked up the rubber cock and teased my rim with it before beginning to push it slowly into me.

"Fuck that's good," I groaned as I pushed the dildo deeper. It burned, but I didn't stop. I knew Jax wanted to watch my ass swallow the full length. When it was all the way in and the flange pressed against my body, I was over-loaded with sensation. Could I really take this and Jax's cock in me?

"Fuck yourself with it," Jax ordered as he gripped my ass cheeks, pulling them apart to give himself a better view. "I want to watch you take it while you think about my cock stretching you alongside it."

I looked over my shoulder at him as I slid the dildo out and began working it in again. "Goddess, that's going to hurt."

He smiled. "I know, but you're such an eager slut you'll take it anyway."

I pushed the dildo in again, moaning as it filled me. I loved it so much when Jax called me a slut. "I will take. I need it. Need you to wreck my ass."

Jax growled and put his hand over mine on the dildo's flange. He tugged, pulling it from my ass, and then forced it into me hard and fast. I gasped as I fought to accommodate it.

"Do it like that," he ordered. "Hard and rough. Fuck your-self like you want me to fuck you."

I obeyed, whining and whimpering as I shoved the dildo in and then pulled it out slowly, relishing the slide of it against my channel.

Jax growled. "Just like that. Imagine me inside you too, stretching you beyond what you think you can take. You'll beg me for more, even though you think it's going to split you in two, because you want me to own you. You want me to treat you like the slut you are."

"Fuck, yes!" I was close. Much more of his dirty talk combined with the dildo dragging over my prostate, and I was going to come. I slowed down my strokes, but Jax snarled at me.

"Don't stop,"

"But I—" He slapped my ass, causing me to jerk and sink down hard on the dildo.

"Keep going, and do not come."

I wanted to protest. To tell him I couldn't hold back much longer. His scent seemed to surround me. I could feel his wolf, and I could so easily imagine fur brushing against my thighs as I straddled him instead of just his human hair. "Please, I... can't."

He spanked me again. "You can hold out because I want you to, and you want to please me."

I did want to please him, and if I could, I'd get his cock inside me and his fangs in my neck. I used my free hand to circle the base of my shaft, squeezing hard enough to make me wince as I kept working the dildo in and out. After what seemed like ages, Jax grabbed my wrist again, stilling my hand. "Are you ready for more?"

"Yes, please. I want to know what it feels like to be stretched wide, pushed to the limit."

He tugged on my wrist until I pulled the dildo all the way out. "Turn around. As fun as it is to watch your hole stretch, I want to see your face when you're stuffed full of two cocks."

My movements were clumsy because my legs shook from holding me up and from the anticipation of being claimed by my mate. But I managed to turn around and ready myself to sink down onto Jax's cock. When our eyes met, he brushed the sweaty curls from my forehead. "You're so fucking beautiful. I couldn't have asked for a more perfect mate."

Warmth filled my chest. This amazing man loved me. Not only that, he thought he was lucky to have me. But I was the lucky one. I'd found a man willing to give me what I craved, a man who respected my desires but also protected me, a man who was willing to tell me when I was wrong but also praise me when I was right. Jax held my gaze as he reached behind me and teased my rim. I bit my lip to hold in a whimper and pushed back, trying to take his fingers inside me.

"Stay still," he ordered. "I'm controlling this. I'll tell you when you get to have something else in that hungry ass of yours."

"Yes, Sir."

He growled, and I was sure he knew how badly I wanted to disobey. I wanted to take his cock in my hand and force myself down so I could be full again. I wanted to ride him until he shot his load deep inside me. But I would wait because I also wanted to be good for him.

He picked up the dildo from where I'd laid it on the blanket. At first, he just teased my hole with the tip while he used his other hand to encourage me to spread my legs wider and sink lower. I sucked in my breath when I felt the tip of his cock brush me too. He continued to tease me with the toy and his own warm flesh.

"Do you know what to do if this is too much for you?" Jax asked.

"I'll use my safeword, but please don't make me wait anymore. I need this. I need to know how it feels."

He tightened his grip on my hip. "I'll give it to you when I'm ready."

I whimpered, hoping he saw the desperation in my eyes. I'd leaned forward to support myself on my arms, but they were shaking so much, they weren't much use. The anticipation was too much. I was sure I'd go insane from it if he didn't fuck me soon.

Finally, he pushed the tip of the dildo inside me and then pressed his cock in next to it. I bit my lip to keep from protesting. Just that little bit was enough to make me certain both shafts were not going to fit inside me.

"Sink down, slowly," Jax said. "You need to be careful. You shouldn't stretch yourself too fast."

I held my breath as I lowered myself. It hurt like hell. Jax was right. I liked having my ass filled, but this was so much, too much. I'd only taken an inch or so, and I was panting, tense and uncertain.

Jax squeezed my hip, and his touch helped anchor me. "You can do this, baby. You can take it all. I know you can. Just go slow and remember to breathe."

I whimpered. "It hurts, but I want it. I want to do this for you."

"I know. You're such a good boy. You'll let me stuff your ass full no matter how hard it is to take."

"Yes, I will. I'm yours. Your slut."

"That's right. Take some more, little slut." I lowered myself a tiny bit more before pausing to catch my breath. A few seconds later, I took another inch or so.

"That's good, baby. Give me a little more. You don't have to take it all, not like you would if there was just one cock inside you."

"I... I want... I want to please you."

"You are, baby. You're perfect."

I was starting to adjust to the fullness. I lowered myself a little bit more. I still felt stretched to the limit, but there was no longer just pain. There was pleasure too.

"That's enough," Jax said. "I want you to fuck yourself now. Ride both these cocks. Enjoy how stretched you are, how open for me. Bring yourself right to the edge again, but don't come."

I rose off Jax and the dildo and then slowly sank back down, taking just a little more than I had at first. I had to move more slowly than I would if only Jax were inside me, but eventually, Jax began fucking into me, and it felt so fucking good to know I could take it. I needed it. I needed to be used, to be fucked, to be allowed to be the cockslut I was.

"So good, Jax. Just what I need. So close... Want to come."

A few seconds later, when I was right on the edge, sure I would spill my seed any second, Jax pulled the dildo out and dropped it on the blanket.

"Take all of me now. Hard and rough, just like you like it."

"Yes," I cried. "Fuck, yes. I want to be yours. Please. Bite me." I worked myself on his cock, tilting my hips so that he dragged over my prostate every time I rose off him. It felt glorious. The extra stretch had been incredible, but all I really needed was Jax—inside me, underneath me, his sent surrounding me. I fought the urge to come, but it was too much. I was overstimulated by his scent, by my need to bond with him. My wolf was snarling to be free. "Can't... Can't wait anymore."

He wrapped a clawed hand around the back of my neck and yanked me toward him as his teeth extended into fangs. "No more waiting. Come for me while I make you mine."

I turned my head to the side. Jax nuzzled me, his beard tickling my neck. Then, a moment later, his fangs pierced me. I screamed as pain and pleasure spiraled through me, sending me over the edge. My hips pumped as cum shot from my cock, making a sticky mess between us.

Jax's knot was starting to swell. It was my turn now. I bit him as he had me and I felt his cock jerk inside me. He was mine. My mate, and everyone would know it. The mate bond fully formed between us, and I felt Jax's pleasure as his climax crested. The intensity was enough to make me come again. As I cried out, the world darkened and then faded away.

When I came to consciousness again, Jax was licking at the wound he'd made on my neck. Once I shifted to my wolf form, it would be healed, but it would leave behind a mark that would let everyone know I'd found my fated mate. Jax would have a matching mark showing he was as owned as I was.

My wolf was anxious to be free, but my brain was so filled with fog I struggled to form words. "Need to shift. My wolf... I need."

Jax lifted me off him, and I rolled to the side. We both transformed, and our wolves nuzzled, licked, and nipped at each other before rolling over and over, tumbling and playing. I wanted to run, but I knew Jax's leg wasn't ready for that, so after our wolves had exerted themselves as much as I thought was good for him, we curled up together, snouts on top of each other's backs, and slept in a little patch of sunlight. No one could dispute that we were mates now. We were bound together, and whatever happened from here on out, we would stay together.

21

JAX

W hen I woke the next morning, Storm was already up and dressed in one of his power suits.

"What time is it?"

"Almost nine."

"Seriously? I slept that late?"

"You are recovering from a major injury."

I remembered everything the previous day had entailed. "And from mating you."

Storm grinned. "That too. How's your leg feeling?"

I flexed it and rotated my ankle slowly. Shifting again had been good for it, and I'd already been able to put more weight on it as we'd returned to the house the day before. If I shifted again today, I'd likely be able to walk on it normally.

"It's fine. Better than yesterday. Are you heading into work?" I assumed he must be since he was dressed for it.

"No, I'm getting ready to tell King and Garrett about what Trent's been up to."

That was not the way I'd planned to start my day. "Why now?"

"When I woke up, I had a message from Corbin.

There's another party tonight, so we've got to move quickly. I've called all my brothers, and they'll be ready to listen to my plan in an hour. I was going to wake you soon."

"Do I get to hear your plan first?"

Storm took a long, slow breath.

"I'm not going to like this, am I?" I asked.

"Possibly not, but I have thought it through. I'm not just rushing into danger to prove I'm as brave as my older brothers. I want to be an active part of this though. And you'll be there with me. I'm going to put measures in place to protect me and Corbin as well as you and Bryce."

"Will you listen to my suggestions and trust me if I say we need to rethink part of the plan?"

Storm considered that. "As long as your suggestions aren't that I stay home and let the bigger, stronger wolves take care of things."

"I want you to have a role in this. You deserve that."

Storm sat next to me on the bed and kissed me gently. "Thank you."

"You're welcome, my mate."

He kissed me again, not so gently this time. When we could bear to pull apart, he told me his plan. He was right. It was well thought out, and based on the crash course I'd had in shifter politics over the last few months, I thought it had a good chance of working. "I'm impressed."

Storm's smile made my heart flutter. "I told you I could do this."

"I never thought you weren't smart enough, cunning enough, brave enough, or anything else that would prevent you from planning this. I only ever thought you let emotion take over when you need to stop and think."

"I do. Mainly because jumping in headfirst was the only

way I got to do anything when I was younger. Otherwise, my brothers would refuse to listen to me."

"This time, you're going to tell your brothers exactly what you have planned, and then you're going to do it."

"And you're going to back me up?"

I laid a hand on his shoulder. "You're my mate, and I'm here for you. I'll always have your back. I support you in this. Yes, it's dangerous. But I know how unhappy you would be if I tried to keep you locked up here. If you tried to go into this without me, I'd be hurt and angry. But you've thought this through well."

He put his hand over mine. "I learned my lesson about that."

"And now you're thinking about your safety and Corbin's."

"And yours."

"And mine." I pulled him in for one more kiss before I went to shower, and Storm called for food to be sent to our room so we could be well-fed when we faced his family.

As we walked downstairs to talk to Storm's brothers, I felt warmth coming through the bond as well as determination. Just before we entered the room, I laid a hand on Storm's back. "I believe in you."

He glanced over his shoulder, and the smile he gave me helped me stay calm as we opened the door and all four of his brothers stared at us.

Shadow was actually in human form for the meeting. From what Storm had told me about their talk before they'd met with Corbin, it sounded like Shadow would support Storm's plan completely. Bryce might question Storm's role in what he'd planned, but I didn't think he'd forbid it. King's expression told me he was prepared to dislike what he heard, but Emerson was sitting next to King and smiling at Storm.

Perhaps he would be a good influence on King. Garrett's expression was perfectly blank, letting me know there was likely a riot of emotion he was covering. I could tell how tense he was from the way he held himself and from the lines around his mouth, but I couldn't be sure how much of his tension had to do with Storm's announcement. Apparently, it was still unclear to Storm how Garrett had known as much as he had about Aidan's plans for a Crown family coup.

"What exactly is this about?" Garrett asked. "I have about a hundred things on my plate for this morning."

"This is about the fact that Trent has been coercing some of our escorts into working for him at private parties at Lucky's, keeping all the money for himself, and, as far as we can tell, Bernice knows nothing about it."

King growled, and Garrett, for once, actually looked surprised.

"I told you we should've gotten rid of Trent months ago," Bryce said.

"And I told you that would fuck everything up with the bears," King snarled. "But I thought someone"—he looked pointedly at Garrett—"was keeping a closer eye on him."

Garrett actually looked contrite, something I'd never seen before. From the shock I felt rolling off Storm, I guessed he'd rarely seen it either.

"I thought I had things covered there," Garrett said, his voice soft. "I suspected Trent was skimming a percentage of the profits, maybe even encouraging the escorts to work extra hours and keeping that work off the books, but I had no idea about any of this. Forgive me."

Shadow tugged on Garrett's arm. When Garrett sank onto the couch next to him, Shadow cuddled against his side. "No one else saw it either except for Storm, and he kept what he knew to himself until recently."

Garrett scrubbed a hand over his face. "It was my job to be watching Trent, not Storm's."

"We'll discuss this later," King said. "Right now I want to hear more about what is going on and how Storm figured it out."

My mate tensed, and I had to resist the urge to touch him. He needed to stand on his own for this.

"First of all," he said. "I need you to promise not to freak out."

King ran a hand through his hair. "I'm getting the feeling that's going to be impossible today."

"At least try," Storm insisted.

Emerson gave King a pointed look, and King let out a put-upon sigh.

"Trent's been texting me for months, insisting we should go out with each other."

All of Storm's brothers—even Shadow—growled, and my wolf made his displeasure known as well. I didn't even like the idea of Trent looking at Storm. I'd barely made it through that awful night at Luciano's without ripping the man apart. I was hoping I might get a chance to do just that tonight. If Trent made a wrong move, I would make sure he regretted it.

"I've known for a while that Trent was up to something more than just pushing us to change the rules and pocketing a bit of extra money," Storm continued. "But I hadn't been able to prove it, so I went out with him."

"You what?" King snarled.

Storm held up his hands. "It's okay. I took Jax with me."

"That does not make it—"

"Hear him out," Shadow snarled. King was so shocked by Shadow raising his voice that he complied.

Storm explained what he'd learned from Trent's phone

call and his texts. He skipped over the part where I'd had to come to his rescue and simply said that one of the escorts had been willing to give him the details he needed, including the information that Trent was holding another of his parties tonight.

"Where is it?" King said. "No matter what it does to our alliance, we've got to put a stop to this. We can't let Trent put our people in danger."

"I know," Storm said. "We don't want to let this go on any longer, but we also don't want to piss off the bears, which is exactly what could happen if we raid a party taking place at Bernice's favorite casino. That's why I have a plan."

"Fuck," Garrett said. "This is even worse than I thought. How did I miss this?"

Shadow patted his leg. "You've been preoccupied. Of course, it would be nice if you told us what's really going on with you."

Garrett didn't say anything else, so Storm continued. "Emerson's friend, Henley, helped me do some investigating. We can't find anything to indicate that Bernice knows about these parties. Everything points to Trent doing this on his own, which means he's not only cheating us and our escorts out of money, he's also cheating Bernice out of the cut she would certainly demand from him."

"Good point," Garrett said.

"Henley helped you?" King asked.

Storm nodded, and King looked at his mate. "Did you know about this?"

Emerson frowned. "I knew he was talking to Henley about business, but I didn't ask for details."

King turned to Storm, clearly about to start another tirade, but Storm didn't let him. I loved seeing him stand up for himself, and I sent reassurance through our mate bond.

"Here's what we need to do. Henley is going to help us wire Corbin and Bryce with mics so we'll be able to communicate with them and also so they can record their interactions at the party. Once the party has gotten started, Jax and I will go in the main entrance at Lucky's and insist on seeing Bernice. She's always there on Saturday nights. That's when she hosts her weekly high roller game. It will likely take some serious persuasion to lure her down to talk to us, but I've been told"—he paused and looked back at me—"that I'm rather good at talking people into things."

Bryce and Shadow both snickered, but King continued to watch Storm like he couldn't believe my mate hadn't stopped to ask his advice yet.

"I'll explain the situation to Bernice and ask for her assistance with Trent. I'll assure her I have the evidence to prove this is Trent's operation and let her know we welcome her dealing with him in any way she sees fit. This way, we get her assistance in stopping Trent, and we've done her a favor by preventing her from looking like a fool since Trent is pocketing money on her turf and she's unaware of it."

King growled. "There's no way I'm letting you—"

"It's actually a really good plan," Garrett said. I could feel Storm's pride at his brother's response. I was sure Garrett's approval meant a lot to him. In many ways, he was a much harsher critic than King.

"You're right. It is a good plan," King acknowledged. "But Storm isn't going anywhere near there."

Storm growled, and I laid a hand against his back. "I'm the one who figured out what Trent was up to, and I'm the one who made the plan. I will be going. Jax will be there to protect me, and Bryce will be there as well, so—"

"Bryce will be focused on Corbin and the other escorts."

"But Jax will be right by my side."

King snarled. "Jax was with Emerson, but he got taken anyway, and Jax and Denny were seriously hurt."

His words would have hurt more if I couldn't feel Storm's love through our mate bond.

Storm growled at his brother, and Emerson glared at him.

King raised his hands in surrender. "I don't blame you, Jax. I'm just saying we can't guarantee Storm's safety."

"He's right," I said.

Storm looked at me like he couldn't believe I'd said that.

"No one can ever guarantee that someone will be safe. Not when they get in a car, or walk down the street, or go charging into a lion's den to attack their enemies. Life is full of risks, but Storm wants to take a calculated one."

King seemed to be pondering my words, but Storm was too worked up to wait for him to respond.

"See. I could get hurt on my way to Tooth and Claw. What are you going to do to solve that? Lock me up here in the house?"

"Like you do me." Shadow stood from the couch and growled.

King looked horrified. "I don't... I thought you liked being here, Shadow."

"I did at first, but I want more responsibility now, and Storm deserves that too. He can do so much more than you let him. I know you want to be our protector, but you can't keep any of us in a bubble."

"I actually agree with Storm and Shadow," Bryce said. "It's time for us to back off. As hard as it is to watch, they can do everything we can do."

King growled. "They're not alphas, and they're not —"

"They're wolves," Emerson said. "And they're smart and strong. I realize I have different limitations as a human, but

Storm's right. He came up with this plan. He should be the one to enact it."

King threw up his hands. "What is happening here? Suddenly everyone is siding against me. You all want me to send Storm into danger. Garrett's taken up with lions and forgotten his duties to us."

Garrett snarled. "I fucked up with Trent, but I'm a wolf, and I know it."

King refused to relent. "My mate was almost killed a few days ago. I'm not sending my little brother into danger."

Storm snarled. "Jax will do everything he can to protect me. He'll watch me closer than anyone else would, even you, because he's my mate."

My mouth dropped open. Had he really just said that? I was shocked but not angry. More than anything, I felt relieved. King was going to find out soon anyway, especially now that Storm and I had mate marks.

Storm glanced back and mouthed, "Sorry."

I couldn't keep from smiling. "I thought you weren't going to be reckless anymore."

Bryce snorted. "As if that would happen."

"Mates?" King said, looking from one of us to the other. "What do you mean?"

Storm gave an exaggerated sigh. "Since you just found your fated mate"—he paused to gesture at Emerson—"I thought you'd understand the concept." He turned and let King see the mate mark.

King snarled, and my wolf readied himself to defend my mate. "When did this happen?"

"Yesterday, just before you gave Emerson your claiming bite, if I'm guessing right."

Color rose in Emerson's cheeks, but he smiled at me and

Storm. "I knew something was going on between you two. Congratulations."

Shadow pulled Storm into a tight hug, and then surprised me by hugging me just as fiercely. Bryce pumped his fist in the air and whooped. Even Garrett congratulated us, although more quietly.

King only stared. "How did I not see this?" He sounded more hurt than angry now, which made me regret that we'd kept it from him because of my stupid fear.

"You've been rather preoccupied for the last several weeks," Storm said, glancing toward Emerson, who'd moved closer to King as if hoping to calm him with his presence. "And even before that, all the shit with the Council kept you from paying much attention to what was going on at home."

King looked around at the rest of his brothers. "Did you all know?"

They all nodded, even Garrett, which answered our question about him.

King looked back at Storm. "Did you tell them?"

"Only Bryce, and I didn't mean to. Our intention was to keep it a secret, but apparently, we weren't very good at that."

King huffed. "Except in my case."

"It was wrong of us," I said, stepping forward. "We should have told you, all of you. Storm was worried how you would react and then I was upset that I'd failed to protect Emerson, but we should have told you anyway. I'm sorry for that."

King studied me for a moment. Then he held out his hand. "Welcome to the family."

That was more than I'd ever expected. I had a mate now, so I wasn't alone, but I was gaining far more than that with King's acceptance. I had a family, a place where I truly belonged.

I shook King's hand, and he shocked me by pulling me in for a hug. "Thank you. That means a lot to me. My parents died a few years ago, and I don't have any other family of my own, so knowing that I'm welcome here—"

"Of course you're welcome," Bryce said, clapping me on the back. "We're lucky to have someone like you watching out for Storm."

Storm shoved at his shoulder. "I'm not a kid anymore."

Bryce snorted. "I hope not, considering what happens when you get a mate mark."

King scowled at Bryce and then looked back and forth between me and Storm. "This is going to take some getting used to, having my little brother mated, but I'm happy for you."

Storm hugged him and they both wiped at their eyes when they pulled apart.

"Now I'm wondering what else I've missed besides this and Trent," King said once he'd composed himself.

"No one else saw what was happening with Trent either, but I have proof now, and I'm going to take care of the problem."

King took a deep breath. "I still don't like this. I can't stand the thought of you putting yourself in danger."

I put my arm around Storm. "There are no guarantees, but I swear to do everything in my power to keep your brother safe. I've seen what he's capable of, and I believe he can do this. He's not asking to take part in a fight. He just wants to be the one to negotiate."

"If Bernice decides she doesn't believe you—"

"She won't," Storm insisted. "I'll see to it."

Garrett stood up next to King. "Let Storm do this. He's obviously been paying more attention than either of us."

"You haven't even been here," King snarled.

"I know, and I'm sorry."

Tension crackled between the two men. But then King put an arm around Garrett and embraced him too. When they let go, King said, "You're all going to start telling me things as soon as you learn them. I can't be the head of the family if I don't even know what's going on."

All of us came together for a group hug then. I felt Storm's warm presence beside me, and I smiled as King put an arm around Emerson and gave him a soft, loving look.

It felt so good to be there, surrounded by a family I'd come to admire so much. They had plenty of differences, but it seemed that no matter what might pull them apart, they would always come back together.

22

STORM

Jax pulled into a parking spot at the casino. He'd driven us this time. Denny was still not completely healed, and we didn't want to risk him or any of the other drivers being involved.

As he cut the engine, I let out a long breath. I could do this. I had to. Corbin and the other escorts who were at the party needed me to succeed so they would never have to deal with Trent again. That was the most important thing, but this was also a chance for me to show King, Jax, and the others that I could handle being involved in every aspect of our family empire.

I understood why King thought I was in danger, but I didn't think Bernice would act against me. Yes, she might withdraw her support of King on the council—thankfully, his position wasn't as tenuous as it had been when Leon had led the lion shifters—but I didn't believe Bernice would dare harm me and risk war with the wolves. They wouldn't win, and she would never have King's support again if she harmed me.

Jax laid a hand on my thigh. "Are you nervous?"

"A little."

He raised his brows.

"Okay, a lot." I didn't want to be, but I couldn't help it. While I didn't think our lives were at risk, there was a lot at stake. Bernice might not want to provoke King to an all-out fight, but she wouldn't hesitate to encroach on our territory if she could. If we didn't hold control of the high-end escort business, someone with far less concern for safety would snatch it from us.

Jax brushed his fingers along my jaw and turned me to face him. "I would worry if you weren't nervous. You need to own those feelings, then set them aside and walk in there like you've never doubted yourself for a moment. You've got this. This is your night to shine and show your brothers you're just as good at being a badass as they are."

"What if I'm all wrong about how Bernice will react?"

Jax shook his head. "You're overthinking things. You've made a plan. Stick to it. We've got contingencies. If we need to, we'll use them. Now isn't the time to change course."

He was right. Even King and Garrett had agreed that appearing like we were doing Bernice a favor was our best option, even if King didn't like the idea of me being the one to do it. I took one more deep breath, then grasped my door handle. "Let's get this over with."

I tried to look casual as I walked toward the casino. I could do this. I could face down Bernice and make sure Trent was punished for what he had done. Before we got close enough to the door to be heard, Jax turned as though he were speaking to me and used his mic to check in with Bryce and Corbin.

When he tapped his ear to silence his mic again, he said. "Things are going as expected."

"If they go as expected for us too, we'll have Trent pinned down with nowhere to go."

When we entered the casino, I stretched up to my full height and settled my shoulders. As I walked across the floor, I felt the warmth of Jax behind me, assuring me that I would succeed.

We reached the door marked VIP Guests Only, and I reached for the handle as though I belonged there. A very young security guard who'd been standing along the wall several feet away called out to me.

"Excuse me, sir. May I see your badge?"

I gave him my most charming smile. "I'm here to see Bernice. I'm a… friend."

"Are you on the list, sir?" the young man asked as he tapped on a tablet screen.

I shrugged as if lists were beneath me. "I haven't the slightest idea, but I'm sure she wants to see me, so I'll just…" I reached for the door again, and the man moved to block my way. Jax growled, but the guard stood his ground. "I'm sorry, sir, but this area is off limits to everyone who is not on my list."

I sighed as though I were extremely put out. "I just explained that I am a personal friend of Bernice. I'm quite sure she will want to see me, and she will be very displeased when she learns I've been made to wait. What is your name?"

I could feel Jax's amusement through our mate bond, and I had to resist the urge to look at him. I had the feeling he was enjoying my performance far too much.

The man looked from me to the door. He was considering letting me in, but he was also concerned what would happen to him if he made a mistake. And rightfully so. Bernice was not the harshest of the shifter leaders, but she was swift to punish disobedience if someone broke her trust. That was why I was certain Trent would be made to suffer for his crimes if I could get her to accept my story.

"I'm Daniel, sir. If you will tell me your name, I'll check the list and see if you're on it."

I could have just given the man my name, but I was playing a role, and I'd decided it was best to drop into it from the start.

"Darcy Powell," I said. Henley had hacked into the casino records, gotten a copy of the list of VIPs, and made me an ID to match one of their names, a man Garrett knew. Garrett had then called Mr. Powell and lured him to another venue for the evening on the pretense of there being an even bigger pot available there.

Daniel found the name I'd given. "I see your name here, sir. Now if I could just see some identification." The guard gave it a cursory glance and handed it back. Bernice would not be pleased if she'd seen how lax he was once I'd given him my name.

"You may go up, sir."

Jax reached to open the door.

"You are perfectly safe to go up alone," Daniel said.

Jax gave him a cold stare. "I go wherever Mr. Powell goes."

"We have the tightest security of any casino in the city, and I assure you the VIP area is—"

"I don't go anywhere without my bodyguard."

"Then I'll need a copy of his ID."

Knowing this could be an issue, Henley had created a fake ID for Jax too. He was much less likely to be recognized than I was, but there was a chance Bernice kept tabs on all the Howler employees, especially the ones who'd been guarding King's mate.

Daniel typed in some information, then handed the ID back.

"I hope that is all," I said. "I'm growing very impatient."

Daniel blushed under my glare. He was definitely new at this. Why would Bernice put someone new on this detail. Unless... whoever was supposed to be there had left for some reason.

"I haven't seen you here before," I said as my hand fell once again to the doorknob.

"I've only been here a few weeks, sir. I'm new to town."

"And already working the VIP access door? That's impressive. Your boss must be very pleased with your work."

"Oh, I'm actually filling in for someone who had to... well, you don't need to know that. Have a good night, sir."

Trent would need someone else to help him with his operation. Was that where the man who should be working the VIP door had gone? Were they encouraging some of the high rollers the usual guard would know to pay for their services instead of filling Bernice's table? That would make Trent's offense much worse.

"Thank you," I said to the nervous young man as I pulled the door open. Jax took it from me, holding it while I entered.

Henley had come through with a map of the casino as well, so we knew to head up the carpeted stairs and then turn left. I took a breath when we reached the door behind which Bernice herself should be presiding over a table of her most treasured clients.

"I believe in you," Jax whispered. His low voice sounded the same as it did when he told me that in bed, and I shivered. But this wasn't the time to think of all the delicious things he might do later to reward me for my success.

When we entered the room, it only took Bernice a second to recognize me. "Storm Howler, what are you doing here?"

"I have information you need, and I'm here to give it to you." My knees felt wobbly. I wanted to grab onto the back of one of the empty chairs, but I stood tall and tried to feel Jax's support as if it could hold me up.

"How dare you interrupt my evening with your nonsense." She turned to the two hulking guards behind her, and they stood, ready to defend her. I'd known her long enough to know she didn't actually need their protection. She was likely far more dangerous than either of them. I was also certain Jax could take out Bernice and her guards. My mate was special like that.

"Get them out of here," she ordered. The guards began to move toward us.

"I can tell you what I have to say right here in front of everyone, or you can speak with me in private. Either way is fine with me, but I'm sure you wouldn't like your family business bandied about by everyone." I glanced around the table, noting that there were numerous shifter groups represented. There was even a human woman. She must be brave as fuck.

Bernice held up her hand, and the guards froze. "You're telling me you have important information to share, yet instead of requesting a meeting with me, you show up here. If King knows something about me, why would he send his pretty boy to do his bidding instead of coming himself?"

I managed to keep my face impassive despite the hammering of my heart. "I didn't say anything about my brother. I said *I* know something you need to know."

Her eyes widened, though she covered it quickly. I'd impressed her, and I could feel Jax's approval through our mate bond.

She glanced at one of her guards. "Take these two to my office and check them for weapons." She turned her gaze back to me. "Make a wrong move, and you'll be shot with enough natcylid you might not survive."

I stared at her coldly. "Don't do anything you'll regret."

"You'll be the one with regrets if you're wasting my time." She gave her attention to the guards again. "Once you've got them settled, send Carl to me."

Jax and I followed the guards without further protest. It sounded like Bernice was going to talk to us once she had someone else to preside over the game in progress. I didn't like the idea of being watched by her two goons, but I had Jax with me, and I was certain he could get us out of practically any trouble.

Bernice kept us waiting for over half an hour. Her guards ordered us to keep our hands on the arms of the chairs where they'd made us sit. The longer I had to stay still, the more agitated I felt, which I assumed was Bernice's intention. Jax looked utterly calm though. In fact, at one point, I thought he might've fallen asleep. I wondered if he could teach me that level of patience. Probably not.

When Bernice finally entered the room, she dismissed the guards, telling them to wait outside. She glared at us as she took a seat behind her desk. "Cross me, and you won't leave here alive."

I smiled sweetly. "Like I told you, I'm here to help."

Bernice snorted. "Start talking."

"First, and possibly not connected to the news I have for you, do you realize there's a sweet little cub who's only been working here for two weeks guarding the door to the VIP area? He says the man who was supposed to be on duty had something else to do."

Bernice visibly tensed. She tapped the microphone in her right ear. "Andrew, confirm for me that Dale is on duty by the VIP entrance." Silence for a moment. "What? Why am I paying you if you can't keep up with your staff better than that? Get the situation corrected. Now." She tapped the mic again and glared at me.

"You're welcome. Now, I have an idea where your man, Dale, may be."

Bernice snarled. "Don't play with me, pup."

I could hear Jax scolding me as clearly as if he were speaking out loud. He was right. I was enjoying myself a little bit too much. "Your nephew, Trent, has been hosting sex parties using escorts from our service as well as others, some of whom are likely underage."

"And this is a problem for me because…?"

"He's holding them in your casinos and keeping all the money for himself."

Bernice growled.

"Ah, I didn't think you knew."

She scowled at me. "What proof do you have of this?"

"He's holding a party in one of your private rooms right now."

"What? He's here?"

"I'm not sure who else is involved from the inside, but it could be Dale. It must be someone, since Trent and his clients are here and you didn't know."

A growl rumbled in her throat. "And I suppose you've been profiting well from this little venture. Why tell me now?"

Jax tensed, and I laid a hand on his arm to soothe him. "Trent hasn't given us a single cent, nor has he paid the escorts he's been bringing to these parties. If anyone else but him is seeing any of the profits, it must be whoever helped him set this up. This is a problem for both of us, and I'm here to help you put a stop to it. I've got some people on the inside, and my guard and I are available to assist you in shutting Trent down."

"I won't need your assistance."

"Apparently you did need us because you were unaware of what's going on right under your nose. That doesn't look very good for a casino owner."

Bernice snarled. "What do you want?"

"Nothing but your continued support of my brother's agenda and the same consideration we've given you. Should you discover something wrong in our house, you'll pass that information along privately."

She studied me for several seconds. "It seems you're a lot more than just a pretty face …" She paused to give me a slow once over, which made Jax growl.

"You're mates, aren't you?" she asked.

I wasn't sure how she knew, but there was no reason to deny it. "We are."

"Congratulations. Follow me to my security office."

As we walked back toward the main floor of the casino, Bernice told off her security chief in a blistering tone, then ordered him to gather a team to deal with Trent.

I glanced at Jax. He smiled as he laid a hand at the base of my spine and leaned down to whisper in my ear. "You're totally a badass."

"You like it?" I asked.

"I'll show you how much once we're back home."

23

JAX

The fact that Bernice allowed us into her security control room let me know that no matter how much posturing she did, she believed Storm's story, and more importantly, she trusted him, maybe even liked him. That would bode well for the future of our alliance with the bears.

Bernice pushed her security chief aside, took over the keyboard he'd been using, and brought up a variety of angles of the room Trent was using on the screens. She quickly found the one where Trent was hosting his illicit party. When I saw the bastard, my wolf snarled, desperate to be free. He wanted to chase Trent down and rip into him.

Another camera showed Bryce with Corbin seated on his lap. He was caressing Corbin's side and whispering in his ear. Possibly they were discussing what was happening in the room, but I didn't think their interest in each other was fake. I glanced at Storm, and he turned to me at the same time. When I tilted my head toward the screen I'd been watching, he smiled and mouthed, "I saw."

I glanced at another screen and couldn't stop a growl from coming out. An older man yanked a boy by his hair, forcing him to his knees. When the boy tried to get away, the man slapped him. If I'd thought their play was consensual, I wouldn't have minded it, but the look on the boy's face told me he did not want to be there, and I'd be shocked if he were over sixteen.

"This needs to stop now." It was all I could do to hold my wolf back. On another screen, a woman was being held down. She was struggling, and she looked terrified.

Bernice snarled a series of orders at the security team, assigning them different entry points to raid the room. "Whatever you do, don't let that fucking nephew of mine escape. He's going to pay for this. If we were inspected by the human authorities and they saw this…" Her words trailed off in a growl, and she turned to me and Storm. "You go in here." She pointed to the entrance closest to Bryce's location. "Get your brother and his companion out of there. This is my business now."

"Not quite yet," Storm said. "Until I know all of my employees are safe and Trent is in your custody, I'm not leaving."

Bernice scowled. "Fine, but do not interfere in my family business."

"Agreed."

Before Bernice could say anything else, the mic in my ear crackled, and Bryce said, "Trent just recognized me. He knows something's up. He headed out the main door. I think he's going to make a run for it, but I can't go after him and leave Corbin."

"We're on it."

"What's going on?" Bernice and Storm asked at the same time.

"Trent spotted Bryce. He's on the run, but I've got him."

"Go," Bernice yelled.

Storm followed me as I'd known he would. I wanted to order him back inside, but I also didn't want him out of my sight. Screams erupted as Bernice's guards raided the party, but Storm and I kept moving. Bryce would take care of Corbin and the other escorts.

We saw Trent near the edge of the parking lot. He headed toward a restaurant that was closed for the night. It was dark as we approached, but I was used to watching for shadows to move.

Trent gave himself away when he reached for his weapon. I was prepared for him. I reached for my throwing knife, which I'd hidden in my boot so well Bernice's guards hadn't found it.

What I wasn't prepared for was Storm. He shifted so fast he was nothing but a blur. He leapt at Trent, and my heart stuttered. Trent likely had his gun loaded with high-powered natcylid bullets. If one hit Storm just right...

But Storm was too fast. He pounced on Trent, and Trent's gun flew from his hand. Storm sank his teeth into Trent's shoulder, but Trent's bear was bulkier, and he threw Storm off.

I had my knife in hand, but I couldn't risk hitting my mate by mistake.

Trent pinned Storm, and I tossed the knife and charged him, shifting partially. Storm turned his head just in time to avoid a deep bite, and with a fierce growl, I grabbed the back of Trent's neck and lifted him off Storm, letting my claws dig into him.

"Never touch my mate again." Trent struggled, but I squeezed his neck, cutting off his air. When he slumped over, unconscious, I tossed him to the ground.

Storm had become human again. He was staring at me, wide-eyed. "Is he dead?"

I shook my head as I became fully human again too. "I pinched a nerve in his neck that cut off his oxygen supply. He's breathing again now, but he'll probably be unconscious for a few minutes."

I heard shouts, and casino security guards began to run toward us. We explained what had happened, and they secured Trent and carried him off. The ropes they used wouldn't hold him if he shifted, but they would slow him down, and I imagined he'd be locked up by the time he regained consciousness.

I removed my jacket and gave it to Storm to tie around his waist since he'd lost his clothes when he'd shifted. My jacket was torn, but it was so large it wrapped all the way around Storm like a skirt.

The guards asked us to follow them back inside, saying Bernice wanted to speak with us. She was conferencing with her security chief when we arrived, so we headed toward Bryce, who was talking to the escorts in one corner of the large room. Daniel, the security guard we'd met earlier, was there too.

"Is everyone okay?" Storm asked when we reached them.

Bryce nodded. "I've got this under control. Corbin, Daniel, and I will make sure everyone has a safe place to go." Corbin stood by his side, and I wondered if they would leave together after everything was settled.

Bernice walked over to us after sending her chief away.

"Trent is secure," Storm assured her.

"Thank you. As much as it pains me to be beholden to a wolf, I appreciate you informing me of Trent's transgressions. He will be severely punished."

"I'm counting on it," Storm said.

"I assume I will not see you in my casino without permission again." Obviously her appreciation only went so far.

"Not unless there's a good reason, like this one," Storm said.

"Then take your mate and get out."

Storm gave her a slight bow. After checking with Bryce once more, we walked to the car. When we were seated with the door shut, Storm let his head fall back against the seat. "We did it. We actually did it."

I took his hand and laced our fingers together. "You scared me to death when you leapt on Trent."

"He was going to shoot you. I couldn't let that happen."

Storm hadn't known I had the knife. I hadn't told him about it because while I'd thought I'd be able to keep it if we were searched, I couldn't be sure. "You were saving me?"

He brushed his fingers over my cheek. "Of course, and you saved me right back. That's what mates do. They protect each other. It doesn't matter who's the strongest or who's the dominant one in the relationship. We help each other."

I pulled him to me for a long, deep kiss. "Storm Howler, I love you, and I'm so proud of how you went in there tonight and followed through on your plan. You're brave and smart and maybe a little too sassy for your own good, but watching you tonight was a privilege and more than a little bit hot."

"You like me as a badass."

"Damn right I do." He pulled me back down so he could kiss me again. I had to pull away after a few seconds. I was determined not to fuck Storm in the casino parking lot, but once I got him home, I intended to spend the rest of the night showing him exactly how happy he made me.

24

EPILOGUE

Three weeks later

Storm

W e'd started opening Tooth and Claw to members on Saturday afternoons. The crowd was quieter, and I usually loved working then, but today I was restless because in a little while, Jax would be picking me up.

I'd booked us the best suite at the Ritz, and we were taking four days off to just enjoy each other. We'd tried to pick an exciting destination, but we'd realized we were going to spend most of our time in a hotel room, so we'd decided to stay in town. Jax had only lived here a few months anyway, so there was plenty for me to show him if we did decide to get out of bed.

I'd wandered down to the bar to distract myself while I waited for Jax to arrive. I ended up chatting with Aisling, a falcon shifter who'd been a regular at Tooth and Claw for years. After we'd laughed about Bryce entering a dance contest the night before despite his lack of rhythm, she said, "Garrett's not been around much lately. I miss seeing him here."

"He's been tied up with some of our other businesses." That was only partly true, but I didn't want to tell her I hadn't seen much of him either.

"Well, tell him if he'd like to be tied up with me again, he should give me a call."

I'd seen Garrett flirting with her before, but I hadn't been sure if they'd actually played together.

"I'll let him know next time I talk to him."

"Or if Bryce is around, I wouldn't mind seeing him either. As long as he doesn't want to dance."

I raised my brows. "You're going to go from one brother to another?"

She laughed. "Is that a problem?"

"Not for me, but it might be for them."

She shrugged. "I'm a switch."

I frowned, did she think… "I know he's really laid back sometimes, but Bryce is a Dom."

She gave me a strange look. "I know, or at least I assumed he was based on the interactions I've seen him have here."

I considered what she was saying for a moment. Wait. She couldn't mean… "Are you saying Garrett's…"

Her eyes widened. "Um… I'm not saying anything. You didn't just learn anything about your brother from me. Holy shit. I had no idea it was a secret."

Garrett was a sub? It was going to take me a while to wrap my brain around that. Working at Tooth and Claw, I'd met plenty of people whose outward appearance or everyday demeanor led people to make wrong assumptions about their preferences, but Garrett was my brother. He'd been part of our family since we'd adopted him when I was fourteen. How had I not known?

Aisling winced. "I'm really sorry."

"No, it's not your fault. He should have told you if he wanted it kept secret. I'm still happy to tell him you'd like to see him again, but you won't say anything about this conversation, will you?"

"Absolutely not."

My phone chimed then. It was Jax. He was by the side door.

"Is that your man?" she asked.

"Yes."

"Then get going and have an amazing vacation."

I couldn't help but grin. "We will."

When I slid into the passenger seat next to Jax, he pulled me to him for a kiss. I gripped the back of his neck so he didn't pull away. I was hungry for a taste of him, since I'd spent far too much of the day thinking about all the things we were going to do this weekend. Jax had been teasing me for days about a surprise he had for me, and I'd ordered several new toys for us to play with.

By the time I let Jax go, we were both out of breath. "Fuck," he said with a harsh exhale. "How am I supposed to focus on driving now?"

If he was as hard as I was, that wasn't going to be easy. I reached down to adjust myself. "You'll just have to manage."

Jax growled, but he put the car in gear and started out of the parking lot.

I skimmed my fingers along his thigh, knowing—hoping, really—that I was going to earn some punishment for taunting him. "When are you going to tell me about this surprise?"

He grabbed my wrist and pushed my hand back into my lap. "Never, if you keep that up."

"Really? Don't you want to follow through with your wicked plans?"

He groaned. "If you don't stop, my wicked plans might involve pulling over and fucking you on the side of the road."

I contemplated that for a moment. I wasn't sure I'd really mind it.

"You're actually considering it, aren't you?"

"Maybe."

He huffed. "You're insatiable."

"I bet you'll manage to satisfy me this weekend."

"Oh, I will. I'm going to make sure you can barely move by the time I'm done with you."

I shivered. "That sounds perfect."

"When we first talked about what we enjoyed, you mentioned wanting to be forced."

I sucked in my breath. I had, but Jax hadn't mentioned it since, so I'd assumed it wasn't something he was into.

"I did. Are you…?"

"I've fantasized about forcing a man for years, but I've never done it because I needed to be with someone I trusted completely and who trusted me just as much."

"I do trust you. You know that."

He glanced at me, and his smile made me light up inside. "I trust you too. I trust you to know that I would never really force you, that the things I might say to you are all a game."

I laid my hand on his thigh again, needing the comfort of contact. "Of course I know that. You always make sure I enjoy everything we do. Is this my surprise?"

"Not exactly, but the surprise is something we could use to fulfill this fantasy."

"It is?"

"Yes."

He didn't say anything else. "Well?"

"I'll show it to you when you get to the hotel."

"What? That's cruel."

"No, I'll be cruel later. Right now, I'm just being annoying."

I growled. "Damn right you are."

He forced me to wait until we were at the hotel, but once we'd checked in, he opened his suitcase and pulled out a pair of cuffs made from what looked like clear plastic.

"These are for our game," he announced.

"Okay, but what about the surprise?"

He grinned as he toyed with the cuffs. "These aren't regular cuffs. They're xekrum."

Oh Goddess. I'd wanted to know what it felt like to truly be helpless to escape. The falcons dealt in black market ones, but I always knew if I tried to get a pair, someone would tell King. "Have you ever used them on someone? I mean, as a game."

"No, but I've fantasized about it."

"Me too." I stepped closer to him and took the cuffs, running my hands over them and shivering as I imagined being restrained and knowing there was no way I could get free until Jax let me.

"You like the idea of being at my mercy?" he asked.

I looked up at him. "So much."

"I want to pretend I was flirting with you, trying to seduce you. You said no, but I forced you into my car and took you home anyway. Once I put you in these cuffs, you won't be able to escape. You'll be mine to do with as I please."

I shuddered. "That sounds so good."

"You'll pretend not to want it, but I'll know you do. I'll be able to tell what a slut you are."

"Fuck yes. I'll be your eager little slut. I love when you call me that."

"Me too, but only as a game, because I also love how free you are to express what you want and how insatiable you are. I never want to stifle that in any way."

I put my finger over his lips. "Jax, you would never do that. The thing that made me fall in love with you was how you appreciate me for who I am, whether that's a slut, a stubborn idiot, or a badass who solves his family's problems."

"You're damn right I do. I think you're incredible."

I ran a finger down his chest and gave him a sultry smile. "Incredible enough to drag back to your lair and fuck into submission?"

Jax

No other man could make me as crazy as Storm did.

Take, my wolf insisted. *Now.* I grasped his chin and forced him to look at me. "Are you ready?"

His eyes widened. "You want to do this now?"

I hadn't planned on it. I'd thought we'd get some dinner and talk for a while, but his teasing had me so hard I wanted to toss him on the bed and take him that second. "Yes."

He walked to the door, put out the Do Not Disturb sign, and closed the safety lock before turning to face me. "I'm ready."

The smirk he gave me had me charging toward him. He gasped when I grabbed his arms and spun him around, pushing him into the wall.

I caught his wrists together at the base of his spine, gripping them tightly. Then I leaned down and spoke next to his ear. "You were flirting with me. You know you were. You want this. You want me buried inside you, fucking you like the slut you are."

Storm struggled so hard he almost slipped out of my hold. Sometimes I forgot how strong he was.

I took his wrists in one hand and slapped his ass with the other. "Stop that."

He struggled harder, and I growled, gripping his neck and letting him feel my claws. "You won't get away from me. Not until I'm done with you."

I pulled the cuffs from my pocket and clicked them shut around one wrist and then the other. "Not even a big bear shifter can break these cuffs, and you're just a little wolf pup."

Storm snarled. I could feel the wolf inside him as he tugged on the restraints, testing them. "Why are you doing this to me?"

"Because I want it, and I know you want it too. I'll have you begging for it soon."

I took hold of his arm and dragged him across the room. When we reached the foot of the bed, I could feel his desire pulsing through our mate bond, and it made my cock ache. This game was everything I wanted it to be, but I knew I couldn't draw it out for long.

I turned Storm to face the bed and used a hand between his shoulder blades to push him down so he was bent over, torso against the mattress, hands trapped behind him, ass tilted up. I undid his pants and jerked them down before letting my claws extend and running a hand over his ass. He gasped when he felt them prick his skin.

"Please. Let me go. Please."

He tried to roll away, but I gripped his shoulders and held him down. "You're mine." I pushed his shirt up out of the way, baring him completely. "This ass is mine. I can do anything to it."

I reached under him, grabbing his cock and stroking it roughly. He whined as he fucked into the circle of my fingers.

"See. You want it, don't you? You're a desperate slut who wants me to own your ass."

"No. Please. No."

I kept going, jerking him off until he was panting. Then I knelt and licked his hole. He shifted and squirmed, trying to get away, but I held his hips in a tight grip. "Stop. Please stop. What are you doing? That can't be right. You shouldn't—"

"Don't tell me no one's ever eaten this ass before. That's hard to believe."

"No. I wouldn't… I never… I'm not a slut. I'm not." He jerked at the cuffs, trying to free himself. He was so good at this. I might believe his protests if I couldn't feel his lust coming through our mate bond.

I tongued and licked him while also using my fingers to open him up. By the time I was ready to fuck him, he was whimpering and begging for more, having forgotten all about fighting me.

Once I'd retrieved a packet of lube from my pocket, I undid my pants, pulled my cock out, and slicked myself up.

"Please," he whined when I pressed my cock against his hole.

"I told you I'd make you beg."

"No. That's not… I don't…"

I slapped his ass. "You do want this. And I'm going to

give it to you. I can't wait to see if your tight ass can stretch enough to take my thick cock."

He tried to turn his head to look at me. "Please don't. It's going to hurt. Your cock is too big to fit in there."

I started to push into him, and he struggled so wildly I had to pin him down with a hand on the back of his neck. "You're going to take every inch of me. If you don't stop your whining, I'll have to gag you."

He whimpered as I worked my way deeper but stayed still until I was all the way in. "That's it. This ass is mine, so get used to it."

"Please," he cried. I wasn't sure if he was protesting or begging, but I pulled out, then drove back in hard enough to jolt him.

"Oh Goddess. That's—"

"What you need." I gave him another hard thrust and then kept working him with a merciless rhythm. We were both panting. Storm began pushing back against me, obviously relishing every stroke

"That's it. Show me how much you want it. Show me what a slut you are for me."

"Yes, please. I'll be your slut. Just don't stop."

"I knew you wanted this."

"Please. I want more. I want you to fill me up, to come in me."

His words almost made me lose it. I took his cock in my hand again and worked him. "Come for me, little slut."

It only took a few strokes before he was coating my hand with his load. I couldn't hold back as his tight ass squeezed my cock, but I pulled out before my knot could lock us together and jerked myself off so I could coat his back and bound hands in cum.

"Goddess, yes," Storm cried. "So fucking hot."

When my orgasm subsided, I pulled the handcuff key from my pocket and freed him. Then I helped him onto the bed and pulled him into my arms.

"Is there anything else you've fantasized about for years but never done?" Storm asked. "Because if it's as hot as this, we need to try it now."

I raised my brows. "Right now?"

He tilted his head in consideration. "Tomorrow at least."

"I'll see what I can do, but I didn't think to pack a sex swing."

"Oh fuck, you want to put me in one?"

I grinned at him. "I do."

"Remind me to call and book us a room at the club for the night we get back."

"Maybe you should wait and see how sore you are then. I have lots more plans for this ass." I pulled him on top of me and gripped his firm cheeks.

He smiled down at me, and I could feel his happiness and his love. "I'm so glad I found you and that we fit together so well."

He wiggled his ass. "Mmm, we sure do."

I gave him a mock scowl. "You know that's not what I mean."

"I know. And even if we didn't do any more kinky stuff, you've already fulfilled the biggest fantasy I ever had: finding a mate I could love and trust who accepted me completely."

I pulled him in for a soft kiss. "I never thought I'd find anyone I could fully relax with. I've been trained to always be on guard, and I still am when we're in public, but when I'm alone with you, you help me turn all that off and let go."

"That's what mates do. They make life better for each other."

"I can't imagine anyone I'd rather be mated to than you. I love you more than I can say."

Storm's smile warmed me all over. "And I love you, my mate."

We kissed again. This time, it was soft and sweet and filled with all the joy I felt through our bond.

Dear Reader,

Thank you for downloading *Bodyguard's Bite*. I hope you enjoyed it. If you haven't read Howler Brothers Book 1, *Claiming Bite*, you can grab it now. Enjoy shapeshifter romance? Try *Wild R Farm* or *Law and Supernatural Order*. And if you like your shifters with a side of mpreg, check out the *Lonely Dragons Club*. I offer a free book to anyone who joins my mailing list. To learn more, go to silviaviolet.com/newsletter.

Please consider leaving a review where you purchased this ebook or on Goodreads. Reviews and word-of-mouth recommendations are vital to independent authors.

I love hearing from readers. You can chat with me on Facebook in Silvia's Salon or email me at silviaviolet@gmail.com. To read excerpts from all of my titles, visit my website: silviaviolet.com/books.

Silvia Violet

ABOUT THE AUTHOR

Silvia Violet writes fun, sexy stories that will leave you smiling and satisfied. She has a thing for characters who are in need of comfort and enjoys helping them surrender to love even when they doubt it exists. Silvia's stories include sizzling contemporaries, paranormals, and historicals. When she needs a break from listening to the voices in her head, she spends time baking, taking long walks, curling up with her favorite books, and hanging out with her family.

Website: silviaviolet.com
Facebook: facebook.com/silvia.violet
Facebook Group: Silvia's Salon
Twitter: @Silvia_Violet
Instagram: @silvia.violet
Pinterest: pinterest.com/silviaviolet/

ALSO BY SILVIA VIOLET

Lace-Covered Compromise

A Chance at Love

Coming Clean

If Wishes Were Horses

Revolutionary Temptation

Of Hope and Anguish

Three Under the Christmas Tree

Needing A Little Christmas

Trillium Creek

Love at Lupine Bakery

Love at Long Last

Love Times Three

Love Someone Like Me

Law and Supernatural Order

Sex on the Hoof

Paws on Me

Dinner at Foxy's

Hoofing' It To The Altar

Wild R Farm

Finding Release

Arresting Love

Embracing Need

Thorne and Dash

Professional Distance

Personal Entanglement

Perfect Alignment

Well-Tailored (A Thorne and Dash Companion Story)

Made in the USA
Coppell, TX
25 October 2021